The Mysterious Case of
NANCY DREW & THE HARDY BOYS

The Mysterious Case of
NANCY DREW &
THE HARDY BOYS

Carole Kismaric & Marvin Heiferman

A Lookout Book

A Fireside Book

Published by Simon & Schuster

New York London Toronto Sydney

CONTENTS

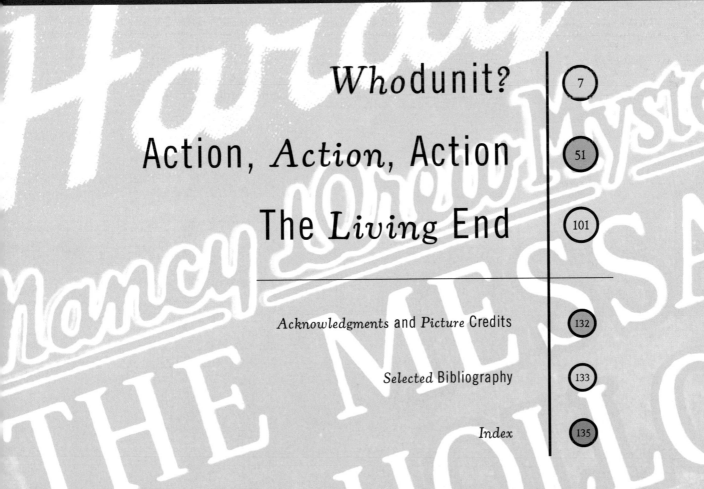

As he spoke, he heard a muffled cry fr
e. Frank wheeled around, just in time
tch a glimpse
asp of two men. Another stranger plung
t from among the trees, hurled himself

Whodunit?

One sunny spring Saturday morning, two bright-eyed boys, Frank and Joe Hardy, hopped on motorcycles and zoomed onto the opening pages of the first detective story ever written for American teenagers. It was 1927, the year Charles A. Lindbergh flew solo across the Atlantic, Babe Ruth hit sixty home runs, and Moulay Hamada, a teenager, was crowned the sultan of Morocco. The Hardy Boys were teenagers out for a ride, unaware that in solving the mystery of The Tower Treasure,

they'd pass up a lazy vacation from Bayport High School to land in a spotlight of fame and fortune. Three years later, at the height of the Great Depression, just after Shirley Temple was born and the first tampons went on sale, blonde rich girl Nancy Drew cracked *The Secret of the Old Clock* and became the liberating heroine teenage girls would shadow to soak up clues about how girls can take risks, live by their wits, and still win the respect of everyone.

Hundreds of whodunits and seven decades later, Nancy Drew and Hardy Boys books still enthrall adolescents longing for escape, independence, and feelings of omnipotence. Four generations of underage armchair detectives have plunked down their allowance money at five-and-dimes, bookstores, and malls to buy close to 200 million volumes of cliff-hanging dramas.

In each new story, page-turning moments of suspense—when life is at stake, when evil is about to gain an edge, when justice must prevail—grab the imaginations of kids struggling through their own adolescent obstacle courses. When puberty hits, whether it's at eight or thirteen, it triggers a hormonal roller-coaster ride of out-of-control passions, alarming physical transformations, and violent mood swings. Preteens can't wait to be teenagers, but once they are, they find out it's not so much fun. Teens are challenged—by parents, society, and themselves—to settle on an identity, but the process is tricky. They are the targets of constant and sometimes conflicting messages. First, there's the shaky feedback coming from their own mutating bodies. Then, there's the revolution at home, as kids try to break loose from the vise-like grip of parental powers. There's school, the educational conveyor belt that's meant to manufacture model citizens but turns out to be a hive of high jinks, peer pressure, and petty humiliations. And on top of all that, as teens are working overtime trying to find and express who they are, the media tidal wave hits them with a flood of trivial options and easy answers, guaranteeing romance, sex, and power to any kid able to pay the price.

Being a teen is a challenge and a thrill, but it's exhausting. Escapism is one way that kids block out the rest of the world and say "Enough!" What gawky, self-critical youth on the road to adulthood doesn't want to take a break from braces and pimples, homework and nagging parents to move into an action-packed world where clues lead to answers, adults don't have all the answers, and teenagers are celebrated for being just who they really are—indefatigable and independent do-gooders who keep the world safe and the scales of justice tipped in the right direction?

Time flies and adrenaline surges when boys crack cases with the Hardy brothers. They're the kind of friends most boys dream of, guys who punch their way out of places with great names like Pirates' Hill or Skull Mountain, and dodge the likes of unsavory crooks like Kitten Cole and Jake

Jomo. Terrifying human screams may punctuate the night, animals may howl and owls screech, but Frank and Joe never lose their nerve. Doubt-free and driven, the boys never fail to corral the bad guys and banish them to jail. The Hardys may find themselves locked in a railroad ice car or an airplane's claustrophobic cargo hold, trapped by a thunderous avalanche or lost in thick fog, but they'll always bounce back—from poison, punches, and sneak attacks—because they *are* hardy boys, luckier and more clever than anyone around them.

Teen detective queen Nancy Drew offers girl readers something more than action-packed adventure: she gives them something original. Convention has it that girls are passive, respectful, and emotional, but with the energy of a girl shot out of a cannon, Nancy bends convention and acts out every girl's fantasies of power. She performs faultlessly as a bareback rider at the circus. Her beautiful larkspurs win first prize at the annual Blenheim Charity Flower Show. She sends secret messages by tap-dancing in Morse code. She reads Chaucer in Old English, and drives her blue roadster with astounding skill. Locked in a room full of spiders, Nancy doesn't get the creeps; she gets out. Her persona—equal parts girl, boy, teenager, and adult—allows her to blossom in a man's world without giving up the

G. Stanley Hall, *bottom left,* invented adolescence. The first American Ph.D. in psychology and founder of the American Psychological Association, Hall debuted his creation in 1904 in a two-volume mix of evolutionary biology and Puritanism modestly titled *Adolescence, Its Psychology and Its Relations to Physiology, Anthropology, Sociology, Sex, Crime, Religion and Education.* Before Hall, the passage from childhood to adulthood was measured in days, weeks at the most, and there were a variety of coming-of-age ceremonies to deal with it. After Hall, the years of teenage turmoil were considered a "separate state . . . the last great wave of human growth."

MASS-produced FUN

Mass-produced tales of violence, adventure, and fantasy, dime novels by the 1860s reached all classes of Americans in all corners of the country.

Life was a struggle for most people in the nineteenth century, and, for many, reading provided one of the few escapes. Satisfying Americans' love of stories in any form, episodic or as parts of ongoing series, turned into big business when advances in papermaking and printing technology made the mass production of reading matter possible. Even twelve-year-old Thomas Edison, whose own life would become a model for future fictional heroes, hawked dime novels from a Port Huron, Michigan, periodical stand on the eve of the Civil War. In 1870, the Novelty Press, a steam-powered, rotary machine, made printing paperbound volumes—pocket to newspaper size, sixteen pages and up—widely accessible and cheap. Story papers (compilations of various action tales) and dime novels (complete stories, staple bound and with soft, pulpy covers) could be mass-produced and shipped across America by the trainload.

In the story papers, tales of phantom horsemen, treacherous Indians, dukes and duchesses, men in iron masks, and poor working girls who turn out to be rich, as well as the adventures of superhero characters like the athletic Frank Merriwell (whose exploits were featured in *Tip Top Weekly*) entertained story-starved readers. Book series, some written by single authors,

some about specific characters or groups of characters, soon followed. The popular rags-to-riches stories written by Horatio Alger Jr., the first of which was published in 1868, compressed all the bright promises of capitalism into pages any boy might read and fueled the imagination and dreams of lower- and middle-class Americans.

In 1888, the first full-color comics came out in America. The best known of these were published in weekly installments in the *New York Sunday* paper and were reprinted in the early 1900s as the first comic books. Eagerly anticipated and read by adults and children alike, comics reached their heyday in the 1930s with classics like *Little Orphan Annie* and *Dick Tracy*. Serial shows on the radio kept hopeful listeners wishing for marital bliss to find *Our Gal Sunday* (1937–59) and chasing villains through mean city streets with the cops in *Gangbusters* (1936–57). When *Amos 'n Andy* (1929–54) vibrated across the country on radio airwaves from 7:00 to 7:15 P.M., normal family life and business activity virtually came to a standstill.

Movie theaters, too, featured serials, which were projected onto the silver screen to growing audiences. The 1914 biweekly installments of *The Perils of Pauline* documented the adventures of plucky heiress Pauline Marvin and inspired a series of copycat adventures like *The Hazards of Helen* and *The Fates and Flora Four-flush*. When movies got longer, Hollywood studios milked the series idea by producing strings of films featuring stars playing charismatic characters like Tarzan, Flash Gordon, and the Thin Man.

Series entertainment found its perfect medium in television. Before TV, 63 percent of Americans were asleep by midnight; by 1951, three-fourths of those with televisions were up late watching the tube. That made for a lot of people: the number of households with televisions climbed from 8,000 in 1946 to 32 million in 1955. Weekly shows like *I Love Lucy* (1951–57) became staples of American entertainment, so popular that department stores were forced to shorten their evening hours to allow shoppers to hurry home and stay up-to-date on life with the Ricardos. By 1959, the average family sat in front of the television console six hours a day, seven days a week, watching live dramas, quiz shows, soap operas, talk shows, news programs, children's shows, and detective stories, each of them divided up into segments punctuated by advertisements, which paid the bills for all the fun.

perks of being a girl and frees her and her readers from a prison of gender expectations.

Nothing diverts Nancy from her mission—solving the mysteries that shroud missing wills, hidden jewels, clever forgeries, heinous embezzlements, and the abandonment of hapless orphans. Outrageous coincidences catapult Nancy through convoluted plots. There's always a chase, a kidnapping, or both, along with an impostor to unmask, an arcane code to crack, or one more sentimental clue to track down through the stock haunts of gothic novels—antiquated inns, castles, cobwebbed attics, dank cellars, secret chambers, and creaky hidden staircases.

It's no wonder that fans read Nancy Drew and Hardy Boys mysteries whenever and wherever they can—waiting for the school bus, sprawled under a tree in the backyard, or hidden under a blanket with a flashlight. The comfort comes from predictable characters whose personalities never change; the fun comes as one volume leads compulsively to the next and make-believe plots begin to crisscross with real life. Mysteries pop up in the unlikeliest places: a penny found on the kitchen linoleum is a harbinger of danger, a locked diary triggers a violent case of curiosity, a familiar bookcase hides a secret passageway. Even the dog's friendly bark sounds a warning. Boring, everyday life turns into an exciting case to be solved, once you start to live like Nancy or Frank and Joe.

These three hyperactive crime busters, who never sit still long enough to read a book themselves, were the brainchildren of straitlaced Edward Stratemeyer. A brilliant entrepreneur who would monopolize the children's literature business of the first third of the twentieth century, Stratemeyer figured out how to crack the code of kids' eternal desire for fantasy, adventure, and mystery, and capitalized on their insatiable need for distraction

by selling them irresistible stories that featured young detectives as main characters.

Born in 1862 in Elizabeth, New Jersey, Stratemeyer inherited his taste for adventure from his father, a German immigrant who had left New York to join the California gold rush. Young Edward grew up in a book-filled house, reading popular boys' fiction, such as Oliver Optic's stories about western exploration, life on the rails, military exploits, and international travel. One of Stratemeyer's heroes was Horatio Alger Jr., the celebrated turn-of-the-century author of 125

Edward Stratemeyer (1862–1930), *left,* ran a fiction factory that produced more than 700 different books in his lifetime. *Above:* Horatio Alger's turn-of-the-century rags-to-riches adventures were immensely popular paeans to the American dream.

popular rags-to-riches tales that had sold 400 million copies by 1920, when their popularity began to wane. Like Alger's boy heroes, Stratemeyer was driven to succeed. In 1876, when he was just fourteen, he wrote his first story, "Dick's Composition." The next year he published his own newspaper for boys, *The Young American.*

Stratemeyer's father warned him that writing was a waste of time, but he was compelled to write. While spending his days clerking in his half-brother Maurice's tobacco store, he worked on stories that

were published in sundry magazines and story papers. In quiet moments, he crafted an 18,000-word boys' adventure story, "Victor Horton's Idea," which he wrote and rewrote until it was published in 1889 in *Golden Days,* a weekly magazine for boys and girls. When he proudly showed off his seventy-five-dollar check from the publisher, his father advised, "Paid you that for writing a story? Well, you'd better write a lot more for them." And write Edward Stratemeyer did. By 1893, he had sold forty-nine dime novels and numerous magazine stories. That same year he began honing his skills as a shrewd and speedy editor for *Good News,* a popular six-cent boys' story paper.

Stratemeyer was in on the ground floor of a burgeoning entertainment industry, cranking out cheap literary distractions aimed at America's growing working-class and immigrant audiences—farmhands, mechanics, shop boys, factory workers—people who craved compelling, escapist stories based loosely on everyday events but pumped up with melodrama. He learned the craft and business of publishing at a company called Street and Smith, where he outlined stories and supervised writers. In 1896, he launched his own story paper, but when that failed, he moved on to write historical fiction, striking gold with *Under Dewey at Manila* (1898), a rousing naval adventure set during the Spanish-American War that hit the bookstores just as Admiral Dewey returned to a hero's welcome. It was so popular—selling 6,000 copies in four months—that it was reprinted twenty-two times, putting its publisher in the black and upgrading Stratemeyer from a hack writer to a fin de siècle superstar whose achievement earned him an entry in the first edition of *Who's Who in America (1899–1900).*

In 1899, Stratemeyer launched the Rover Boys (1899–1926), a series that ran until 1926 and featured not just one boy hero, but three: Dick, Tom, and Sam, schoolboys who traveled to different locations to find adventure and sometimes unraveled a light mystery along the way. Shortly before Horatio Alger Jr.'s death in 1899, Stratemeyer realized a lifelong dream when he was asked to finish the last Alger stories in the long-lived series he had adored as a child.

Before he learned to type, the champion of kids' series wrote out his stories longhand. But even turn-of-the-century technology couldn't keep pace with the jet-engine speed of Stratemeyer's imagination. He penned outdoor tales, hunting and camping sagas, and sports, circus, and theater stories. Had he not written under thirty pseudonyms, Stratemeyer would surely have become a household name. In 1905, he came up with his own blueprint for success, which turned out to be one of the great successes in the history of American publishing. Instead of working feverishly as an author to make a living, why not come up with story ideas and outline the plots, farm out the writing to hungry professionals, and then sell the combined effort to publishers while holding on to all the rights? He hired his friend Howard R. Garis to write the first books of the Tom Swift series (1910–41) under the pseudonym Victor Appleton, and as Lester Chadwick, Garis wrote Baseball Joe. As Roy Rockwood, Stratemeyer produced Bomba the Jungle Boy. Ever seeking to expand his empire, Stratemeyer had no compunctions about switching gender, either. He outlined, edited, and produced girls' books under Waspy women's names: Laura Lee Hope was responsible for the Bobbsey Twins (1904–92), while Margaret Penrose penned Dorothy Dale (1908–24) and the Motor Girls (1910–17). As Helen Louise Thorndike, he presented the Honey Bunch series (1923–53) and as Alice B. Emerson he introduced Ruth Fielding (1913–34). Stratemeyer's

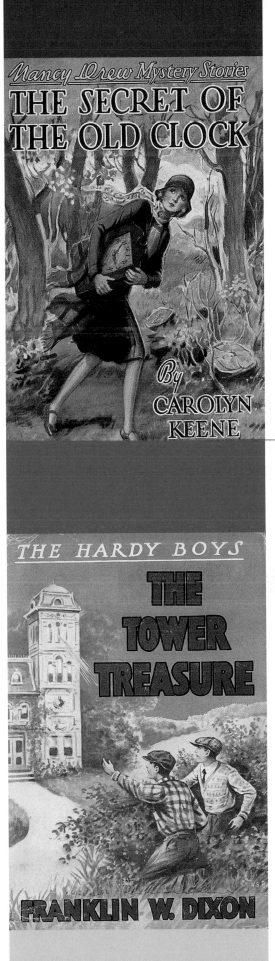

The first books in the Hardy Boys and Nancy Drew series have been best-sellers since their first publication. *The Tower Treasure*, published in 1927, had been reprinted ninety-three times by 1979. *The Secret of the Old Clock* (1930), the most popular Nancy Drew book, had been reprinted 114 times by 1979.

Before World War II, most high school boys bought little more than shaving gear. After the war, prosperity turned teens into a market to which you could sell Cokes, clothes, candy, and cars. By the end of the 1940s, American adolescents were munching 190 million candy bars every week, along with 130 million sodas, 230 million sticks of gum, and 13 million ice cream bars. Radio advertising aimed at juveniles jumped from $600,000 to $7 million over the decade. Television, in turn, painted a bull's-eye on every American teen, and by 1957 the adolescent market was valued at upwards of $30 billion.

publishing concept had been used to produce story papers and dime novels for a mass audience, and echoed another business model, the assembly line, which mass-produced affordable consumer products. The Stratemeyer Syndicate became an assembly line of writers and editors creating mass-market series books for children, turning youthful fantasies into affordable realities. Stratemeyer's timing was perfect. Sales of Syndicate books took off, and other publishers, looking for new adventure series to capture the attention of American boys and girls, followed suit, quickly publishing new series for kids.

From 1910 to 1930, Stratemeyer, the "Father of the Fifty-Center," and his Syndicate kept up with the demand, averaging over thirty new titles a year for up to thirty-one separate series. Stratemeyer, who himself miraculously still found time to dictate three or four books a year, established guidelines for his Syndicate writers to follow. The recipe called for twenty-five chapters per book, each ending with a cliff-hanging episode. There was to be no touching or kissing, and no upsetting violence; in fact, no character could be knocked unconscious more than once per book, no matter how convenient a plot device. Action had to be intense enough to require exclamation marks galore. From conception to publication, a Syndicate book, which Stratemeyer thought of as "safe and sane" reading, was produced in about forty days!

Action, action, and more action kept Depression-era readers in such a state of escapist euphoria that *Fortune* magazine declared, "As oil had its Rockefeller, literature had its Stratemeyer." So effective was his Syndicate that in 1926, 98 percent of kids in an Illinois survey named a Stratemeyer character as their favorite, and, until 1940, the Syndicate produced about half of the most popular juvenile series books in America.

In the 1920s, business at the fiction factory was so brisk that Stratemeyer had to place classified ads to find new writers. He sought professionals who could, under tight deadlines, write readable stories based on the detailed two-page plot outlines that he dictated to his trusted editorial assistant, Harriet Otis Smith. At one time, he had eleven writers across the country cranking out 200-page books every month. Stratemeyer knew that while his real authors would come and go, if they wrote under pseudonyms, their brand names could live on forever.

Stratemeyer Syndicate writers thought of them-

Anthropologist Margaret Mead, *below top*, was twenty-three when she traveled to American Samoa to find out whether nature or nurture most influenced the behavior of adolescents. In 1928, in her best-selling *Coming of Age in Samoa*, Mead refuted G. Stanley Hall's theory that teens' turmoil and frustration were universal, part of a phase written in the genes. She portrayed Samoan teenage life as noncompetitive, "replete with easy solutions for all conflicts," and characterized by playful sexual activity before marriage.

Leslie McFarlane, *above,* the first Franklin W. Dixon, wrote quickly. He could finish a Hardy Boys book in less than three weeks.

The first Carolyn Keene, Mildred Wirt Benson, *below,* authored twenty-three Nancy Drew books. She wrote over 100 other childrens' books, including the Penny Parker series.

selves as "spooks." Happy for the money they were paid—fifty to one hundred fifty dollars per book—writers signed away all their rights, and were forbidden by contract to use their Stratemeyer pen names for other books. They were also discouraged from submitting manuscripts to Syndicate competitors. But Stratemeyer was a good boss, because he understood how to keep writers happy—he sent them steady work, advanced them money when they were strapped for cash, and sent them Christmas bonuses and praise throughout the year.

The Syndicate became known for its school-age superheroes. Bomba the Jungle Boy (1926–38)— kidnapped as a baby, ever searching for his inordinately rich parents—sniffed narcotic jungle flowers and climbed trees, aping Tarzan. Explorer Don Sturdy (1925–35), raised by two bachelor uncles, donned pith helmet and riding boots and explored lost cities and tombs of gold. Girls' book series were flourishing, too; from 1910 to 1930, ninety-four new series starring girl wonders were introduced in America. Stratemeyer was already producing series books for girls, specializing in characters who were a far cry from the goody-goody, domestic antics of *Little Women.* The Moving Picture Girls (1914–16) relocated to Hollywood when their prominent stage-actor father, who had lost his voice, found success starring in silent movies; the Outdoor Girls (1913–33) launched guerrilla wars against Boy Scouts and Girl Scouts, beating them out at kite-flying contests and drill-team activities. Meanwhile, Ruth Fielding (1913–34) became a 1920s favorite because she ran her own film company—writing scripts, producing movies, and starring in them— and juggled a successful Hollywood career with the demands of everyday life. By 1920, girls' series accounted for 30 percent of all Syndicate sales.

Always looking for yet another new angle for a

Once, a teen's major concern was getting a date to the prom. In the 1990s, one-third of eighth graders report having used illicit drugs. Experts now say that the amount of time it takes to get through adolescence is the longest it's ever been and is getting longer. For girls of the nineties, the physical changes that mark puberty begin to appear more than two years earlier than they did at the beginning of the century. At the other end, the age at which most adolescents leave home has steadily risen over the course of the century, from between sixteen and eighteen to roughly twenty-one.

Fitzgerald, Willa Cather, and Somerset Maugham. McFarlane knew that covering banquets and club luncheons for a small-town newspaper wasn't going to turn him into a famous writer, so he answered an ad in the trade journal *Editor and Publisher*:

*Experienced Fiction Writer Wanted
to Work from
Publisher's Outlines*

On April 29, 1926, he received a letter from Edward Stratemeyer, whom he'd never heard of:

All of the MSS we handle are written to order for us, on our own outlines and casts of characters, the author simply "filling in" as it were. . . . For these stories . . . we pay one hundred dollars each. . . . If . . . you care to tackle one of these, please let me know. . . . But I should want to see four or five sample chapters before giving an order to complete a MS.

Soon after, a few sample series books arrived, including one about deep-sea diver Dave Fearless, written by McFarlane's childhood idol, Roy Rockwood. McFarlane was stunned. He realized that Roy Rockwood was as fictitious as the characters he wrote about, and, furthermore, that anyone could be Roy Rockwood—including himself. But McFarlane overcame his disappointment when he figured out that if he spent part of his day writing juvenile literature as a hack, he could earn one hundred dollars for each book and devote the rest of his time to serious writing. McFarlane wrote two sample chapters of a Dave Fearless book, passed the test, and got his first assignment.

When another Dave Fearless assignment came in, McFarlane quit his newspaper job and headed for the Canadian backwoods to live in a cabin, breathe the mountain air, and write his heart out. Six months later, McFarlane noticed with alarm that Stratemeyer's latest Dave Fearless outline didn't contain the usual plug for the next book in

series, Stratemeyer had the brainstorm in 1927 to fuse the tried-and-true, nineteenth-century adventure saga with an adolescent version of the newly popular detective mystery. "Detective stories are as interesting to boys as [they are to] grown folks," he wrote to Grosset & Dunlap in 1927 when he sent a list of titles for his proposed series. "I prefer two boys, brothers, as heroes. . . . The Keene Boys, the Scott Boys, the Hart Boys, the Bixby Boys, etc."

No matter what they would be named, what Stratemeyer really needed was the right writer.

Leslie McFarlane was a twenty-three-year-old reporter working the hotel beat for a Massachusetts newspaper. He remembered reading Stratemeyer books as a small-town Canadian boy, and idolized one of the Syndicate's authors, Roy Rockwood. By high school, he was soaking up the more sophisticated fiction published in H. L. Mencken's *Smart Set* magazine, stories by F. Scott

PIMPLES

ACNE AND ALL OTHER EXTERNALLY CAUSED

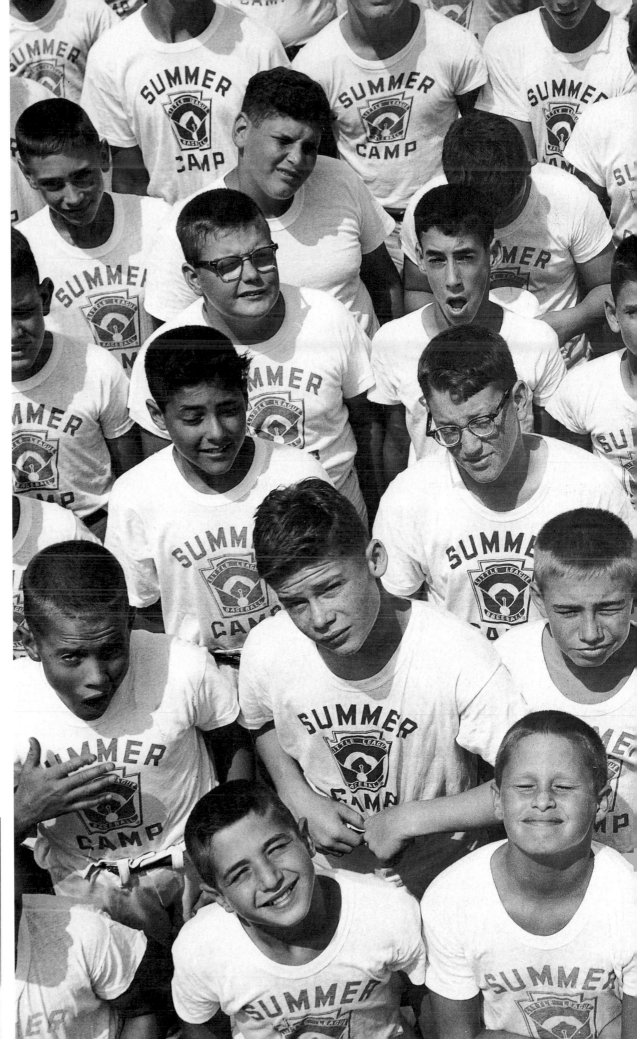

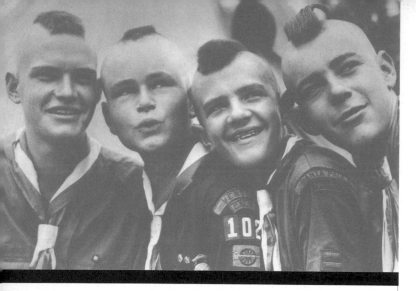

When teens start to smoke, pierce their body parts, or decide that life's not worth living without an expensive pair of sneakers, the knee-jerk reaction of adults is to blame peer pressure—the kids' friends talked them into it. Life-and-death needs for pop-it-beads, teased hair, or platform shoes come and go; the trick is to learn how to resist and still be considered cool. And peer pressure is not necessarily always negative—teens talk each other out of smoking, dropping out of school, or joining gangs, too.

the series. He was out of a job! Weeks passed. Finally, a letter from Stratemeyer arrived:

> *I have contracted for a new line of boys' books to be issued in cloth at a cheap price. . . . For these we pay $125 each. They will be mystery stories, the doings of two lads, sons of a noted detective. I want three yarns for publication in the Spring. Would you like to tackle the bunch as soon as the next Dave Fearless is finished? If you can put them through at the rate of one every three weeks, I will mail cast and outline for No. 1.*

The two-page, single-spaced outline followed, with suggested bits of dialogue, the merest hint of locales, some situations spelled out in detail, and plot telegraphed in a rat-tat-tat rush of words.

> *Boys at school—various doings—Frank and Callie—days pass. Mr. Hardy returns—tells important secret. The auto thief, a criminal named John ("Red") Jackley—called Red because of his fondness for red wigs—is under arrest. . . . "And by the way, he was once a railroad man and worked not many miles from here," remarked Mr. Hardy.*

Knowing that it was his writing that would set the tone for the series and bring these new charac-

ters—the Hardy Boys—to life, McFarlane felt that they somehow deserved better than the slapdash treatment inane Dave Fearless had been getting from him.

McFarlane wrote the first nine Hardy Boys mysteries with plots that took place in chronological order, season by season, intending them to be read in sequence. He wrote under the pseudonym Franklin W. Dixon, a name that to this day triggers authorly images in young boys' and grown men's minds. Even when his fees slid to eighty-five dollars a book during the Depression, he kept on writing, a spook who eventually ground out an estimated two million words for the Syndicate over twenty years, in between writing his own novels, articles, television and radio plays, and movie scripts. Finally, in 1946, while in Nova Scotia directing a documentary film for the National Film Board of Canada, McFarlane mailed his last Hardy Boys manuscript, *The Phantom Freighter,* to the Syndicate with a short note stating that he was too busy for further assignments. No one from the Syndicate seemed to care, and sixteen other men and women each became Franklin W. Dixon, for a while.

By mid-1929, almost 116,000 Hardy Boys mysteries had been sold, and their success made it logical for Stratemeyer to create a counterpart girls' detective series. He sent a plot summary to Mildred Wirt, who'd been helping the Syndicate save the faltering Ruth Fielding. She was only twenty-five when Stratemeyer threw a bigger challenge her way: to write *The Secret of the Old Clock,* featuring a pretty, sixteen-year-old girl sleuth, Nancy Drew.

Born in Iowa in 1905, Wirt was a girl who had hated dolls, was good at sports, preferred boys' books to those written for girls (she devoured Horatio Alger stories), and spent her childhood

outdoors. The first woman to earn a master's degree from the University of Iowa's journalism program in 1927, Wirt believed nothing was off-limits to her. "My parents told me I could do what I wanted, as long as I was willing to work for it," she recollected years later. A feisty Midwesterner, Wirt knew as a child that she'd grow up to be a writer; in fact, she'd tell anyone who'd listen that she'd be a *great* writer. At twelve, she'd won a silver badge when her first story, "The Courtesy," was published in *St. Nicholas Magazine;* other stories soon followed in denominational papers such as *Lutheran Young Folks* and *Our Young People.* Tales about adventurous, independent young women were to become her specialty.

Before Stratemeyer created Nancy Drew, most girls in American fiction were oppressed and self-righteous—agreeable, meek, delicate, stay-at-home types, wide-eyed orphans who possessed immaculate virtue. While the books about them were of a higher literary quality than typical mass-market series books, which were primarily aimed at boys, the characters, even if they felt a streak of independence, bowed to convention when they met a handsome, sophisticated older man. There was *Rebecca of Sunnybrook Farm* (1903), who seemed destined for a remarkable career that sadly eluded her when, at seventeen, she married an older man. A relentlessly upbeat *Pollyanna* (1913) skipped through life "glad, glad, glad" about everything, despite her dead parents, bitter aunt, and a life-threatening injury.

One of the most treasured literary girls of the era was tearful, saintly series book heroine Elsie Dinsmore, who first appeared in

For teens, a supposedly "fun" activity as simple as dancing offers an opportunity to test out complicated feelings about being male or female, as well as a chance to see whether they can measure up to dancing the jitterbug, a slow fox-trot when the lights go down, or the grind.

THE NEW TEEN WORLD

Until the 1930s, most adolescents worked for a living on farms, in factories, or at home. Ambition had no meaning for kids, and, though in the throes of puberty, they certainly weren't given special status just because their bodies were maturing. Parents picked out their clothes, friends, hairstyles, and futures. With no detours allowed on the road to adulthood, girls were destined to become homemakers, boys breadwinners.

In the years when the Hardy Boys and Nancy Drew were cracking their first cases, only kids from prosperous families could afford to go to high school. For poor and immigrant families, secondary school was a luxury. Not only did they need their sons' and daughters' wages to survive, but many also worried that high school would give children "ideas" that would make them dissatisfied with their lives at home. The Depression pushed lower-class kids out of work and into high school. In 1900, 11 percent of American youths were enrolled, and by 1930 the number had jumped to 51 percent. In 1940, the figure stood at 73 percent. The haves and have-nots began to rub shoulders and turn to each other for advice, ideas, and approval.

In 1941, *Life* magazine described this group as youngsters who "speak a curious lingo, adore choco-

were buying a new breakfast cereal. There might be prosperity, but there was no peace. Monsters lurked everywhere. In science-fiction films, pod people threatened to destroy democracy and free will, while in Washington, watchdogs sniffed out communists threatening the American way of life. Nervous adults did everything they could to fit in, to conform, but some teens didn't—they wore blue jeans and tight, shrimp-colored sweaters, chain-smoked, drove fast, danced hard, and mocked the values that they knew were hard to escape.

The beat of rock 'n' roll drove the sound track for the new youth culture, where teens starred in versions of their own lives portrayed in movies like *Blackboard Jungle*. The teen market, a $9 billion enterprise early in the decade, went through the stratosphere, topping $30 million in 1957, the year in which the Soviets launched *Sputnik*. Adult Americans now had two more reasons to be nervous.

By the 1960s, youth culture had come into its own. Many teens took to the streets in open rebellion against the American mainstream—no way they'd sign on for a middle-class rat race, a life divided into little boxes of conformity at home, at work, in school, or in bed. Seventy-seven million baby-boomer teens bought birth-control pills, body paint, vinyl miniskirts, and lava lamps, along with enough pot to keep one out of ten students stoned in class. Teenagers watching TV saw John Kennedy, Martin Luther King, and then Bobby Kennedy, icons all, assassinated. But it was the violent images from Vietnam that stopped polite intergenerational conversation around the dinner table. As soon as American youths questioned whether it was right to fight a war, no authority was sacred. Maybe communes made more sense than families; maybe women could toss off the double standards surrounding sex. Maybe God *was* dead. What was certain was that the cultural balance was shifting.

In the past, friction between parents and young adult children was thought to be temporary. In 1970, Richard Nixon tested that assumption and created an unbridgeable gap when he ordered in the National Guard to silence war protesters at Ohio's Kent State University. Four students were killed. Protests grew so widespread, so loud, that even Congress couldn't block out the noise. In 1971, eighteen-year-olds, old enough to die for their country and pay taxes, finally received the right to vote and an equal voice in running the country.

late milkshakes, wear moccasins everywhere, and drive like bats out of hell." It was not to last, however. World War II put an end to the fun, as 35 percent of high school students dropped out to work in defense plants, factories, and local businesses. Even as the word *teenager* came into widespread use, sacrifice became the accepted way of life, and gasoline, chocolate, sugar, nylon stockings, and chewing gum were rationed. On the home front, the new word's subjects put aside frivolity to tend victory gardens, sell war bonds, knit sweaters, and collect scrap metal.

When the war ended and prosperity catapulted teenagers—along with everyone else—into a charmed world, families and schools began to lose their influence and power over teens. Kids refused to give up the independence they'd tasted during the war, when they'd been left to fend for themselves by parents who had to fight overseas or work hard in war industries. Now, in peacetime, and with money to spend, no consumer group was ever as conspicuous or as clearly targeted by marketers. While parents were building dream homes in suburbia, teens built a world of their own, a culture of youth driven by popularity and governed by peers, new rules, and a singular passion—to be cool.

In the 1950s, the heat of the cold war made coolness cooler. If A-bombs and H-bombs could smother good times with a blanket of fallout, why mow the lawn, stick to curfews, pray to God, or duck and cover? The prosperous postwar world could self-destruct while you

1867 and whose popularity seemed to grow with her physical and emotional suffering. In one book, she contracted brain fever. Other episodes saw her handsome father, consumed by a deranged obsession with his daughter, threaten to banish her to a convent, and, in one exquisitely pathetic passage, force her to sit at the piano for hours until she fainted, hit her head on the side of the instrument, and bloodied her pale curls and snow-white dress.

Girls who took their noses out of books found other girl heroines in similar trouble. Starting in 1914, moviegoers flocked in record numbers to the biweekly serial installments of *The Perils of Pauline.* At the end of each episode, young Pauline Marvin was routinely left struggling with savage Indians, trapped in a Chinatown opium den, or hanging by her fingertips from the edge of a steep cliff. Fans who returned to the movie theaters two weeks later got to see Pauline saved by her manly stepbrother/suitor, Harry, only to head off in disaster's direction one more time.

Mildred Wirt, writing as Carolyn Keene, set out to make Nancy Drew more than a helpless victim waiting for the right guy to come along. By 1930, when the three breeder volumes that kicked off the series—*The Secret of the Old Clock, The Hidden Staircase,* and *The Bungalow Mystery*—were published, American women had come into their own. They had been voting, fighting for social causes, living on their own in cities, working side by side with men, and drinking hooch in speakeasies for a decade. For these changing times, Wirt created a contemporary character and a seductive world that Depression girls could aspire to. She knew that Nancy had to both ring true *and* fulfill girls' dreams of independence, so she gave Nancy the qualities that Wirt herself felt she lacked—good looks and a lot of dates—and enough freedom to get around without getting the wrong kind of reputation. In

other aspects, Nancy turned out to be a lot like Wirt herself—confident, competent, and totally independent, quite unlike the cardboard character that Stratemeyer had outlined when he first dreamed up Nancy Drew.

It took about three months for Wirt to transform what had been outlined as a generic Midwestern town filled with stock characters into a universe of glamour and intrigue, and to create a character with whom any adolescent girl would want to trade places. According to Wirt, Stratemeyer gave her one direction when he hired her: "He said you can snap your fingers at literary content, but keep up the suspense." Legend has it that Stratemeyer, who had made his fortune balancing Victorian morality against the emerging excitements of modern America, was disappointed with Wirt's first manuscript. However, in a letter to her, he wrote that he liked what he had read, and after her second book, he sent her a Christmas bonus in addition to her $125 paycheck.

Nancy Drew Mystery Stories were launched on April 28, 1930. Two weeks later, on May 10, Edward Stratemeyer, the most successful man in juvenile publishing, died unexpectedly of pneumonia at the age of sixty-seven. He had written 150 books, outlined 600 to 700 others, and launched 125 original series. The two cents per

From Charlie Chan, *opposite left,* to Charlie's Angels, *opposite right,* every generation anoints its own favorite private eyes to define evil and triumph over it. In 1924, Charlie Chan started his fight against crime on the page before he took to the screen in 1926. In 1927, the sophisticated Philo Vance joined in, followed over the years by Sam Spade, Philip Marlowe, Nero Wolfe, Mike Hammer, Travis McGee, Columbo, Magnum, and Spenser. Teen detective Nancy Drew helped create an audience for female sleuths like Janet Darling, Nora Charles, the big-haired Charlie's Angels, Jessica Fletcher, Kinsey Millhone, and Kate Fansler.

snapping of twigs. For an instant he lay

nless. With every muscle taut he listened

to tell from what direction the sound

coming. The noise ceased. Straining

TAKE-CHARGE GIRLS

At thirteen, Joan of Arc (1412–31), *below left*, heeded saints' voices telling her to do a man's job—fighting off English invaders—and was ultimately burned at the stake for her efforts. Nancy Drew is fearless, too, in *The Message in the Hollow Oak* (1935): when she and her posse give chase to a gang of thieves, Nancy proclaims with a smile, "I feel like a modern Joan of Arc leading her warriors to battle."

Dorothy, introduced in *The Wonderful Wizard of Oz* (1900) by author L. Frank Baum, was immortalized by Judy Garland, *below middle,* in the 1939 film version. Dorothy was a teenager living on a pleasant but dull Kansas farm until a tornado whisked her and her dog, Toto, to a magical world of Technicolor adventure. Nancy's dog, Togo, first appears as a bull terrier in *The Whispering Statue* (1937) and over time was magically transformed into a Scottish terrier.

By the time Peggy Fleming, *below,* turned nineteen in 1967, she had racked up five national figure-skating championships, two world titles, and was soon to capture a gold medal at the 1968 Olympics. Like the athletic Nancy Drew, she was no slouch when it came to winning honors.

volume that he averaged in royalties for each book sold added up.

Stratemeyer never got the chance to see Nancy Drew blossom into the most popular character in kids' series fiction. In the depths of the Depression, the series racked up record sales. The 6,000 books sold at department stores like Macy's during the 1933 Christmas season prophesied Nancy Drew's stamina and success. By 1938, Nancy's shapely sales figures were nearly twice those of the Hardy Boys.

When Stratemeyer died, leaving an estate estimated at half a million dollars, his various publishers panicked—the Syndicate was the source of half of their juvenile titles. Stratemeyer's wife, in ill health herself, was in no position to take over the empire. Into the breach stepped his right-hand editorial assistant, Harriet Otis Smith. Smith kept the business running while Stratemeyer's daughters, Harriet and Edna, looked for a suitable buyer for the family business. When no one materialized, Edna expressed their reluctance to take charge in a July 13, 1930, letter:

> My sister was here for the day yesterday and together we went over many details. There were many disappointing angles to selling the business and in spite of ourselves it looks as if we must carry on.

The sisters, who both lived in New Jersey, moved the Syndicate office to East Orange. Smith, who preferred life in New York, quit, leaving Edna Stratemeyer and Harriet Adams to run the business. Harriet, who had studied English at Wellesley College and written a few articles for local newspapers, and Edna, who had never read a Hardy Boys book, were at the helm of a thriving family empire that they could neither sell nor abandon. Though they each had a lot to learn, for a while it was almost business as usual, because their father had left behind enough story ideas and plots to keep writers busy for two years. By

mid-1932, the sisters were well along in their learning curve and had added six new series to the nineteen that were already moneymakers. They shared the work of dealing with business matters, plotting stories, hiring and supervising ghostwriters, editing, and rewriting the manuscripts.

In the past, writers had loved working for the Syndicate because Stratemeyer edited from a distance and with a respect for their work. His daughters, however, were running a business in the midst of the Depression and had to take a tougher line. They slashed writers' fees, asking Mildred Wirt, for example, to take a cut in pay, from $125 to $75 per book. "That wasn't enough to make it worth it," Wirt told her new bosses, so the Syndicate hired Walter Karig to take over as Carolyn Keene for *Nancy's Mysterious Letter, The Sign of the Twisted Candles,* and *The Password to Larkspur Lane.* But his books were not as successful as Wirt's, and soon she was back in the fold.

By this time, Harriet Adams had begun to make greater editorial demands on Syndicate writers. Instead of her father's breathless two-page outlines, she insisted that writers follow her more elaborate outlines, which included specific chapter endings. Some writers bridled at her creeping editorial control. Her earliest letters to Wirt, for instance, made polite requests, asking her to watch her colloquialisms and mind the length of her manuscripts, but by the end of the decade, Adams's suggestions had become more critical in tone and content. In a July 1938 letter, Adams responded to Wirt's manuscript for *The Clue of the Tapping Heels:*

> We like the tale, which moves along easily. We miss colorfulness of characters and events. This boat disaster is realistically described, but outside of this the reader has to supply his own ideas of clothing, scenery, weather, and times of day to a large extent. These matters are not essential to a mystery plot, of course,

Mildred Wirt recognized that she and Harriet Adams had two different Nancys in mind. Adams instructed her to "make the sleuth less bold. . . . 'Nancy said' became 'Nancy said sweetly,' 'she said kindly,' and the like, all designed to produce a less abrasive more caring type of character."

But Mildred Wirt, who had authored twenty-three Nancy Drew mysteries in all and considered herself "just a hired pen" who wrote "as well as she could," went on writing as Carolyn Keene until 1948 and *The Ghost of Blackwood Hall.* Remarried, and now known as Mildred Wirt Benson, she returned in 1953 for one last go at Nancy Drew in *The Clue of the Velvet Mask,* which was initially turned down by Grosset & Dunlap due to what the company regarded as its poor quality. Its beginning and end were rewritten by Harriet Adams.

When Edward Stratemeyer set the Hardy Boys and Nancy Drew series in motion, he was well aware of changes going on in American culture, including the nation's growing obsession with crime. Newspaper headlines and talking-picture newsreels screamed about sensational crimes, bloody rubouts, and organized evildoings. Prohibition had turned drinking a casual cocktail into a federal offense. Real hoodlums, like Chicago's Al Capone and John Dillinger, and fictional ones, like Edward G. Robinson's Rico in *Little Caesar* (1930) and Paul Muni's *Scarface* (1932), were transformed by the media into insolent super-

but do add charm to any story. We shall tuck in a few phrases here and there to bring out these points.

Three years later, Wirt, who had penned fifteen best-selling Nancy Drew mysteries to that point, received a letter commanding her to follow the dots to a suitable yarn:

Will you stress that Nancy is sensible, level-headed and very keen, but also sympathetic, kind-hearted and lovable. Bring out the devotion between father and daughter. . . . We have made long footnotes in order to give you clues to characterizations. . . . The outline is very detailed and we trust that you will be able to write the story with ease.

heroes. A golden age of detective and crime fiction dawned, featuring books like Dashiell Hammett's *Maltese Falcon* (1930) and cheap pulp-fiction magazines such as the *Black Mask* that titillated readers, mostly men, with lurid, stylish stories about private eyes, gun molls, and corrupt cops. Ever shrewd, Stratemeyer took the public's fascination with crime and repackaged it for an underage audience, melding the beloved, old-fashioned adventure tradition with the heat generated by gritty tales of modern crime. What Stratemeyer couldn't have predicted was how keenly Frank and Joe Hardy and Nancy Drew would touch another nerve in young audiences of ten- to fifteen-year-olds, kids who were just as eager to test out their new identities as "teenagers" as the breakthrough teen detectives were to tackle a new crime.

Adolescents are the perfect audience for books in which slightly older teen characters have one close call after another and rise above challenges that come their way. Frank, Joe, and Nancy are fictional peers unencumbered by the Sturm und Drang of real-life adolescence, teens who can be admired for their confidence, focus, and power; emulated for their independence; and celebrated for their ability to zero in on excitement. The Hardy Boys' bravery and Nancy Drew's self-assurance are pure inspiration for kids whose lives are defined by changes and confusion, whose growing bodies often feel like haunted houses. Kids who want to break away from adult control envy how mobile Frank, Joe, and Nancy are. Teens bewildered by the complexities of their passage into the adult world happily while away hours in the idyllic worlds of Bayport and River Heights. Like iron filings drawn to a magnet,

OTHER BROTHER ACTS

The Jackson Five (clockwise from bottom: Michael, Marlon, Jackie, Tito, and Jermaine) began singing in 1964 and were later spotted by Gladys Knight, who introduced them to Berry Gordy Jr., founder of Motown Records. The brothers' 1970 single "I Want You Back" hit No. 1 on the *Billboard* chart, and twelve Top 20 hits followed. The honors weren't only musical: Congress cited the Jacksons in 1972 for their "contribution to American youth."

The Kennedy brothers—John (Jack), Robert (Bobby), and Edward (Teddy)—come from America's most famous political family. Like Fenton Hardy, their father, Joe Kennedy, strongly supported his boys and taught them to back one another up on the football field, in politics, and in life. When JFK became president in 1960, he named Bobby attorney general. After Jack was killed in 1963, Bobby threw his hat in the presidential ring in 1968, but was gunned down, too. Next it was Teddy's turn, but the Massachusetts senator withdrew after questionable actions made the public doubt his character and morality.

The Righteous Brothers, Bill Medley and Bobby Hatfield, weren't real brothers like the Hardys, but met in the 1950s as members of the Paramours. In 1962 they set out as a duo, singing what was sometimes contemptuously called "blue-eyed" soul. But these two white guys seemed to get it right, and they inspired one black listener, hearing their act one night, to praise them as "righteous brothers." The name turned to gold when, two years later, they recorded "You've Lost That Lovin' Feelin'." More hits, including "Unchained Melody" and "(You're My) Soul and Inspiration," followed until 1968, when the pair stopped being full-time "brothers."

Frank and Joe are well behaved compared to Leonard, Adolph, and Julius Marx, who are much better known as Chico, Harpo, and Groucho. Zany punsters, the Marx Brothers put on and put down bureaucracy, pretension, and the cultural lunacy that surrounded them, in thirteen movies including *Animal Crackers* (1930) and, their most famous, *A Night at the Opera* (1935).

kids who are just developing their own personal values cling to books about teenagers whose job it is to make the world a fair and better place.

What made the Hardy Boys and Nancy Drew so cool, and keeps them popular today, is not only who they are and what they stand for, but what they aren't. The characters escape the bondage that keeps most teenagers toeing the line. They're never trapped by petty chores, curfews, or the short leash of meager allowances. Frank and Joe don't feel even a twinge of sibling rivalry. Nancy Drew is so self-assured that she doesn't concern herself with what other people think of her. The teen sleuths never get yelled at, because most of the time they aren't naughty. They're not slaves to pets, organized religion, fads, or peer pressure. They're not joiners; the 4-H, the Y, church groups, the Scouts have nothing to offer them. Because these teen detectives live so relentlessly in

the present, they have no regrets about the past and no worries about their futures.

Frank and Joe Hardy have staved off the aging process for seventy years by living in a time warp that rejuvenates them with fast-paced investigative action. Their mother, Laura—who's seldom seen, and, when she is, mostly worries about her sons or packs them lunches—once had other plans for Frank and Joe, nudging them to become lawyers and doctors. But, after they helped their dad crack several tough cases and racked up some impressive rewards, the boys were encouraged to follow in private investigator Fenton Hardy's footsteps. Like other Stratemeyer Syndicate boys—the Rover Boys, Tom Swift, the Speedwell Boys, the Radio Boys, the Moving Picture Boys, the X Bar X Boys— Frank and Joe are adventurous and virtuous lads.

The Hardys' love of adventure and keen sense of justice is in their blood. Their father, a retired

THE HARDY BOY

New York City detective, though just over forty, is youthful and strapping, with graying hair, a stentorian voice, chiseled features, and blue eyes. A firm disciplinarian when the boys were younger, Fenton Hardy now sits back to see how their confidence and self-esteem mirror his own celebrated talents and unerring professionalism. Even though he's often called away on investigations— to solve crimes for corporations and government agencies as well as private individuals—the spirit of tall, dark, handsome Fenton sets the standards and the masculine tone for the Hardy household.

Whether picking up Dad's slack or investigating cases of their own, Frank and Joe are inseparable. They're together almost all of the time and are so close that they can read each other's thoughts. Best of all, they always have someone to talk to.

ARE *you* MAN *enough?*

For more than sixty years, American teenage boys have known what it takes to be a real man—to win like a man, lose like a man, and "take it" like a man. Males must be aggressive, patriotic, responsible, and enjoy sports. They must never, ever cry, back down, or ask for directions. And they learned it all from a big, Iowa-born actor named Marion Morrison, better known as John Wayne.

No one epitomized American manhood quite like Wayne did. Solitary and strong, his on-screen persona radiated masculinity. Director Raoul Walsh, who discovered Wayne, said it well: "The sonuvabitch looked like a man." Director Howard Hawks said that Wayne moved "like a big cat." Wayne stated his philosophy in *The Alamo* (1960), a film that he starred in, produced, and directed: "There's right and there's wrong. You gotta do one or the other. You do the one, and you're living. You do the other, and you may be walking around, but you're as dead as a beaver hat."

Hollywood has regularly served up variations on the Duke—first Robert Mitchum and Victor Mature; then Clint Eastwood, Sylvester Stallone, and Arnold Schwarzenegger, with more sensitive sorts like Gregory Peck, Kevin Costner, and Mel Gibson tossed in. But Wayne, the archetype, held his ground. When he died in 1979, Japanese newspapers proclaimed that "Mr. America is dead," and his spirit still touches every adolescent American male in some way, no matter how old he is.

Of course, boys have masculinity models other than actors—fathers, athletes, soldiers, policemen, clergymen, and even politicians have a place in defining American manhood. In a world run by men, where men made the laws, ran the businesses, built the buildings, drove the cars, and painted the paintings and wrote the great books of Western literature, being

John Wayne (1907–79), the rugged star of 179 movies, topped the list of America's most-admired men for fifty years.

a man meant being powerful, no questions asked. Maleness was fairly straightforward: war was male, athletics were male; muscles, facial hair, power, duty, loyalty, patriotism, and camaraderie all were male.

Once women's liberation redefined femininity and gay liberation raised even more questions about sexuality, defining masculinity became more complicated. Why weren't guys becoming schoolteachers, secretaries, airline stewards? Why didn't guys cook dinner, do the laundry, sew on buttons for themselves, or fuss over the furniture? Why weren't they allowed to raise their children, touch one another, have women friends, and express their feelings? Why didn't men cry? By the 1970s, some men had started to see the downside of being in power, and they started taking a good look at themselves and society's definitions and assumptions about manliness. In the eighties, some confused and disoriented men began carrying around their dog-eared copies of *Iron John* and *Fire in the Belly*, hoping to relearn—or at least come up with their own definition of—what masculinity was all about. Younger men, born after the cookie-cutter model of masculinity was challenged, had the advantage of growing up in a time when gender roles were not quite so rigid or taken for granted. For the first time, they had the chance to learn a new history of mankind in classes like Dartmouth College's "The Masculine Mystique" or, if they went to the University of Richmond, one intriguingly titled "Testosterone: Asset or Liability?," which posed a question that men had never before considered.

Although separated in age by a year—in the earliest books in the series Frank is sixteen, Joe fifteen—in many ways the boys are twins, equals who live for each other. In looks and spirit Frank is dark, Joe is light. Frank's the logical thinker; Joe's the hotheaded, impetuous one. But if one of them is knocked for a loop in a fistfight or dangling perilously from a trapeze, his brother is there to rescue him. Neither Frank nor Joe needs to be perfect as an individual, because together, as a team, *they* are perfect.

The Hardy Boys have each other, their father, and a colorful gang of pals, all ready to sign on for adventure and, when necessary, to play rough, even though they're the kind of boys who wash their hands before dinner. They're men's men, untroubled by women who, if they were part of the action, would only slow it down because they would demand an emotional involvement the

Hardys are not ready to explore. With no girls to worry about, they're free to be action heroes, never in doubt about their ability to perform. Girls make the boys nervous, especially Joe, because their feelings toward the opposite sex are confused. In *The Missing Chums* (1928) Joe's flustered, and it shows:

> *"Oh, do come in," said Iola coaxingly. . . .*
> *"Let's go," muttered Joe, tugging at Frank's sleeve. He was incurably shy in the presence of girls, especially Iola. . . .*
> *Iola tried to make conversation with Joe, whose answers were mumbled and muttered. . . .*
> *"Why, what's the matter? I thought you liked Iola Morton."*
> *"That's just the trouble—I do," answered Joe mysteriously, and Frank wisely forbore further inquiry.*

The Hardys are boy-sized teens who routinely overcome grown crooks, thugs, and other big lugs

the REALIST who RULED storyland

Harriet Adams, shown with two fans in her East Orange, New Jersey, headquarters in the 1950s, took over the Stratemeyer Syndicate, her father's business empire, in 1930. Even without any business training, she ran it profitably for nearly fifty years.

As a woman in control of a million-dollar enterprise in the 1930s, Edward Stratemeyer's eldest daughter, Harriet Stratemeyer Adams, proved herself as exceptional a business mind as her father had been. Adams is sometimes criticized as the controlling woman who, through her revisions, zapped the life out of the Nancy Drew and Hardy Boys series, but, in truth, no single person took a more active role in keeping Nancy Drew and the Hardy Boys alive through the decades.

Graduating in 1914 with a major in English from Wellesley College, Adams wanted to join her father's business, but he felt women did not belong in the workplace and only permitted her to do light editing from her New Jersey home. In 1915, when she married her father's stockbroker, Russell Vroom Adams, Edward Stratemeyer made her quit working altogether, feeling that she needed to invest her time into building a family.

Four children and fifteen years later, Adams returned to the Stratemeyer Syndicate, having spent her time away writing pieces for her local Sunday school and women's club newsletters. A year after her father's death in 1930, she and her younger sister, Edna, took over the Syndicate. They were essentially learning on the job, but their efforts kept the Syndicate on track, and it launched three new series by 1931. While her sister worked on series plot outlines from home, Adams concentrated on planning and writing new titles and forging business deals with publishers. When the economic realities of publishing during the Depression hit, Edna and Harriet dropped many of the Syndicate series, from twenty-nine in 1930 to thirteen in 1935.

As America entered World War II, Harriet took over the day-to-day operation of the Syndicate. Edna, newly married to Charles Wesley Squier in 1942, departed New Jersey for Florida, retained her half of the business and weighed in on all major decisions, but allowed her sister to run things on a day-to-day basis. When wartime rationing was instituted in 1943, Adams cut the series list again, so that by 1944 only five series survived. Her most controversial decision—to revise and update the Hardy Boys and Nancy Drew Mysteries—was a massive undertaking that would occupy her for the rest of her life. Her contributions to Nancy Drew's character in particular made a huge impression on the series. From the 1930s and 1940s, when Adams and her sister outlined the basic plots, and from the 1950s to the late 1970s, when she outlined, wrote, or edited almost every manuscript, Harriet exerted near total control over Nancy's attributes and defined the limits of her world. Saying that Nancy was modeled after the Wellesley motto *Non ministrati sed ministrare* ("To minister, not to be ministered unto"), Adams controlled everything from Nancy's hemline to her disposition. Late in her life, Harriet Adams claimed to have written fifty-five of the Nancy Drew Mysteries and seventeen Hardy Boys books, and maintained that Nancy Drew had remained popular because "the stories are fast moving, exciting, and have a high moral tone. No vulgarity, no profanity, no sex, yet each contains a good mystery, holding the reader's interest from page one to the end."

Outside of the Syndicate, Harriet was the kind of woman Nancy might have grown into. A member of the League of the American Pen Women and the New Jersey Women's Press Club as well as an active participant in the Red Cross and the Girl Scouts, Adams was a ubiquitous community figure. She traveled frequently, visiting East Asia, Europe, Africa, and South America for pleasure and as research for her series books.

In 1982, Harriet Adams died of heart failure while watching *The Wizard of Oz* for the first time. It seems fitting that the last thing she saw was Dorothy, another strong-willed girl, embarking on a journey down the yellow brick road.

because they are so adept at boxing and jujitsu. They understand the superiority of strategy over brute strength. It's the scientifically planned trajectory of a well-placed punch that knocks out the bad guys.

Two bantamweight bundles of young manhood, Frank and Joe drive matching black-and-silver motorcycles. They are sharpshooters, expert drivers and divers; they ride horses, ice fish, and pilot airplanes. They're good auto mechanics who have mastered Latin, sign language, and various secret codes. Together, they're a dream team, but it's Frank, the older brother, who's usually mentioned first and who does most of the driving. He has most of the ideas and acts as the master planner and leader. Frank's quick, razor-sharp mind reasons things out before he makes a move. Though he has a tendency to be modest and cautious, to keep things to himself, when this Hardy lad springs into action, he's worked out all the angles down to the tiniest details. A Scorpio with a clever mind and a good-natured face, Frank may have small feet (he wears a size-eight shoe), but he's tall and handsome and is blessed with straight, black hair and deep, dark eyes. Frank balances his brains with brawn. He's captain and quarterback of the football team, a pitcher on the baseball team, and is a member of the gymnasium club. Off the playing field, he can throw his voice, play the ukulele, administer first aid, and twirl a mean lasso. He's a natural actor who gets the boys out of danger in *The Secret Panel* (1946) by passing himself off as a moron and by dressing up as a woman named Professor Ima Dodo in *The Secret Warning* (1938). He's been an honor student at Bayport High since 1927, except for the year that he dropped out because of a mysterious illness. And when he was well enough to go back to school, he luckily landed in the same class with his younger brother.

Impulsive Joe is a bashful hunk, a 125-pound, good-hearted Aries who has a special interest in ornithology. Among the Hardy Boys gang, Joe's known for his sleight-of-hand feats and card tricks, for being the guy with a cool sense of humor, pink cheeks, curly blond hair, and his mother's

OTHER MODEL DADS

President Franklin Delano Roosevelt (1882–1945), *below left,* was a father figure to millions of Americans when the Great Depression and World War II threatened every family in America. His reassuring "fireside chats," broadcast on the radio and heard by American families relaxing after dinner, helped to generate support for his progressive New Deal programs.

When wartime hero General Dwight D. Eisenhower (1890–1969), *below right,* was elected president in 1952, he shouldered the responsibility of protecting Americans from communism, the cold war, and the evils of big government. The nation's postwar commander in chief—an easygoing, pipe-smoking, golf-playing man—kept the peace and led America through two terms of unprecedented prosperity.

A major force in America's civil rights movement, the charismatic Reverend Martin Luther King Jr. (1929–68), *opposite left,* preached equal rights for black Americans and nonviolence with a passion that spoke to both black and white America. His rousing "I Have a Dream" speech, delivered at the Lincoln Memorial during the 1963 March on Washington, called for freedom, justice, and integration.

Americans so loved the warm smile and familiar voice of B-movie star and television celebrity turned politician Ronald Reagan (1911–), *opposite right,* that they elected him president twice. The presidency was another role in which this immensely popular conservative stood for family, hard work, and self-reliance.

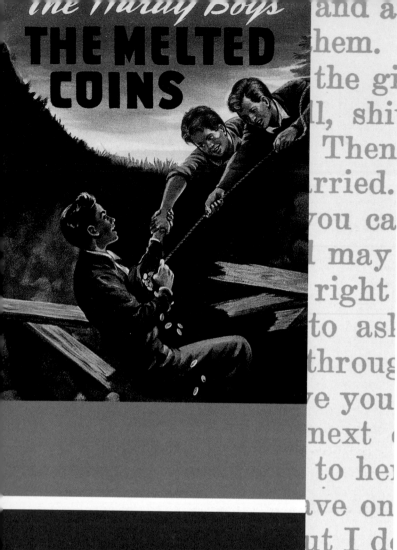

THE MELTED COINS

The Hardy Boys

sparkling blue eyes. Quick on his tiny, size-six feet, Joe, too, is celebrated for his athletic prowess; he plays shortstop for the Bayport High baseball team and holds the record for the longest run in the history of the football team. He's the brother most likely to take chances, so he's the one most likely to be bopped on the head or to unwittingly lead someone else into danger. In general, Joe defers to Frank's better judgment, but in times of trouble, he's the better shot. When the Hardy Boys cruise Barmet Bay in their boat, the *Sleuth* (which they bought with reward money), Frank counts on Joe, the better pilot, to know every inch of the tricky coastline. Same goes for when they have to deal with fires in Bayport; in his brief life, Joe has memorized the location of every fire alarm box in town.

> "I am Nancy Drew," said the girl quietly.
> "I know you are Nancy Drew," mimicked the stranger. "I've seen you go flibberty-jibbet in your auto many a time. When I was a girl, girls stayed home and learned to cook and sew and mind their own business, not to go gallivantin' around in swell autos and waited on hand and foot. I declare I don't know what the world is coming to."
> "If you have come here to lecture me, would you mind waiting until I have finished my luncheon?" Nancy asked.
>
> Nancy's Mysterious Letter *(1932)*

Teen detective Nancy Drew is nothing like most young girls—boy-crazy, always on the phone, morbid, mooning over unicorns, or subject to fits of uncontrollable giggles. This lithe, Wasp supergirl is under control, a plucky and fearless, humble and generous, charming young lady who *never* fails at what she sets out to do. Nancy's not quite a knockout, but she's attractive for sure, with a crown of blonde hair framing her heart-shaped face and sparkling blue eyes. Her cheeks are rosy and her complexion fair, except when she's blushing from praise for her accomplishments.

A clotheshorse with an ever-expanding wardrobe, Nancy acts out every girl's desire for material goods—she has everything, from berets to strapped stiletto heels. With a hefty allowance and charge cards at River Heights's finer emporiums (Burk's Department Store, and Taylor's, too), Nancy can find a snappy outfit for every occasion. If there's diving to be done, count on Nancy to have the perfect rubber suit, flippers, and Aqua-Lung. She looks ultrachic no matter what she puts on: three-quarter-length tailored dresses, flowered crepe gowns, long scarves, pastel frocks for afternoon teas, red slickers, and, by the 1980s, designer jeans.

Everyone loves Nancy—girls, boys, the cops in River Heights, down-on-their-heels spinsters, even the hardened criminals she hunts down grudgingly come to respect her. Nancy's a celebrity who gets invited to a luncheon in her honor at the White House in *The Mystery of the Ivory Charm* (1936), but fame never goes to her head. Nancy's ruled by her brain and rock-solid values.

Like Sleeping Beauty and other classic fairy-tale heroines, Nancy is motherless, and has been since the age of three. But she has not only learned to take care of herself and her dad; she also plays parent to hapless victims of misfortune. Many girls secretly entertain fantasies of rescuing people in need and making their lives happy—Nancy does it daily. Righting wrongs, allaying fears, and specializing in restoring wealth to its rightful claimants, she willingly suffers physical pain in the cause of righteousness, though she's no martyr. A courageous girl, she'll never give in to anger, fear, despair, or a moment of moral doubt.

Nancy is unflappable and observant. Yet, at the same time, she's always running, darting, bolting, springing, bounding, a symbol of energy and freedom. Long before Filofaxes and Day Runners, Nancy organized more in a day than most people

Nancy Drew could thrive because, like many heroines in children's stories, she was mother-less—left to define independence for herself and saved from an emotional tug-of-war she might have had with an overbearing mother, like the mother-daughter relationship portrayed in *Mildred Pierce* (1945).

manage to cram into a week. It's no surprise that she has trouble falling asleep at night. She's efficient and always prepared, not like the proverbial Girl Scout, but just like a successful, sophisticated girl detective needs to be. She tucks a neatly packed overnight case in the trunk of her car, with two changes of clothes, pajamas, a robe, toiletries, and, in summer, a bathing suit. And Nancy always carries her birth certificate; she's a sixteen-year-old going on forty.

Some people think she's sexless, but virginal Nancy is simply innocent of lust or any notion that men have an upper hand. She has no romantic fantasies, and after her first flirtation with Ned Nickerson, no tingling sensations when they twirl around the dance floor. "Someday," she muses from time to time, but Nancy's clearly not ready to make a commitment to her "special friend." She might love fixing up other people and reuniting separated couples, but she'd rather solve a mystery than waste time on a date. Nancy's been raised to take men for what they are in her world—sometimes helpful, sometimes trouble-some, but more often than not, criminals. She's usually more capable than they are; no wonder they tie her up, gag her, lock her in closets, and knock her unconscious.

Nancy may be a threat to some men's masculinity,

but not Carson Drew's. A wealthy, world-famous criminal lawyer, Carson Drew is the *perfect* dad. He's a tall, dark, and handsome widower with a few hobbies—bowling, collecting antique firearms, growing roses and radishes—and no social life. Carson lavishes Nancy with ego-boosting praise to encourage her precocious independence and proffers professional feedback and advice. There's no need for Nancy to succumb to girly whining; she's got her father's ear and trust, a set of car keys, and an ego so strong she can afford to worry about other people in need rather than get lost in self-absorption. That's why Nancy can come home late (as long as she calls) and, even in the earliest of her cases, could head out of town as long as a chaperone tagged along. Mr. Drew, secure in his single-parenting skills, learned a long time ago to support Nancy's addiction to detection.

Out in the "real world," Nancy fiercely protects her father's name as much as she takes advantage of it, and she doesn't hesitate to volunteer his high-priced services gratis to deserving people. Nancy turns defensive when someone says something bad about her dad, and is stricken with terror when she fears that his life is in peril. The father-daughter bond is strong; Carson has no wife, Nancy has no mother. In fact, the two of them seem more like husband and wife than parent and child—Carson doesn't flinch when his attractive daughter playfully runs her hands through his wavy hair. When the two Drews flirt shamelessly, which they often do, they're unaware of the dark psychological undercurrents that kept twentieth-century shrinks' couches warm. Without Nancy, Carson would be a boring lawyer counting his billable hours. With her, though, he is half of Drew & Drew, and no generation gap can rend their partnership.

Nancy's hard to top, a goddess in disguise, a girl whose talents are legendary. With a precision and elegance that defies most teens, Nancy can whip up a dress or interpret a Chopin étude with subtle understanding. She can repair a damaged painting so perfectly that an expert can barely detect it, and she learns to fly so well that she awes her instructor. Maybe it's Nancy's photographic memory that makes quoting Archimedes second nature. And while she never spends a day studying in a classroom, she passes an exam in archaeology after one night's cramming, gets the lead in many school plays, and even graduates from high school in the series' third book, *The Bungalow Mystery*. A self-starter, Nancy loves to learn on her own, to bone up on psychology, underwater photography, auto mechanics, and art, becoming adept enough, to everyone's amazement, to render a crook's face perfectly for the cops.

Nancy's no tomboy, but she loves all sports, too. She's great at golf, excels at tennis, is a sure shot with a gun, and is a Ping-Pong champ. She's mastered ocean fishing, bobsledding, and water ballet. With not an awkward bone in her body, she dives like a swan and swims superbly. Her superior athletic abilities identify her as a twentieth-century woman who knows both the benefits of physical fitness and the thrill of competition.

In fact, Nancy's whole world is bathed in a blue aura. It's her signature color; her eyes are blue, she's decked out in blue clothes when she first appears, her garden is filled with blue flowers, and her shiny roadster is blue. It's not the blue that stands for boys or sadness—Nancy's blue is the cool blue blood of American aristocracy. She's a member of the River Heights Country Club. When she's not traveling the world and checking into first-class hotels, or when she's in between cases, Nancy Drew does her share of charity work. When she lunches at fancy restaurants and quaint local inns, she's quick to pick up the check, never making anyone less fortunate feel uncomfortable. True to her class, she's conservative, apt to get

smug from time to time, to look askance at lower-class, exotic, or ethnic people—until she reminds herself it's wrong to jump to conclusions. And for all her upper-class advantages, Nancy never dreams of abusing privileges or taking a dime for her sleuthing work.

If Nancy weren't free to dart around the River Heights hills and dales in her trademark cars, she'd be a lot less astonishing. Early on, she's in command of a blue roadster—later, it's a convertible, sometimes yellow, sometimes maroon—and she can park in any tight spot. She inspires admiration, not jealousy, because she's been packaged with a split personality meant to spur young girls to independence while reminding them of some of their traditional female roles. Sure, Nancy can fix a car

It's hard to imagine what adolescence in postwar America would have been like without the automobile. For teens in the 1940s and 1950s, cars meant privacy and necking and more, if you dared, although supposedly no nice girl ever did in those days. Sure, there were front porches and loosely chaperoned parties and hayrides, which were nice if itchy, but nothing held a candle to the family car or, even better, your own souped-up jalopy. Then came the bikini in 1958 and the birth control pill and *Lady Chatterley's Lover* in 1960, and America seemed ready to go on what *Reader's Digest* called "one vast, all-pervading sexological spree." At home, church, and school, teens were still told it was wrong to express themselves sexually outside of marriage, but in the locker room, in movies, and on television, the message was "join in the fun."

OF COURSE I'LL BE PROUD OF YOU, KIRK-- BUT I'LL BE AWFULLY LONELY IN THE MEAN-TIME!

or a boat's motor with a bobby pin; she can roll herself down the side of a mountain without getting a scratch, wrangle free of bondage ropes, and dominate every man on every page. But Nancy still relishes her cup of tea with tasty watercress sandwiches, and looks smashing in an evening dress.

Dusted with privilege and blessed with a strong will, Nancy thrives on breaking rules. She fascinates most girls (and some boys) because she's not like them at all. Nancy lives free of doubt because she's got power. No worries about not having breasts, no fears of getting pregnant, no embarrassment about being too tall or too thin, no anxiety over not having dates. No competition, no fighting, no cutting school; no eating disorders, no jealousy.

Americans rely on institutions such as the Boy Scouts, Girl Scouts, and the YMCA (*above*, a 1957 marksmanship lesson) to instill "good values" and character in young boys and girls.

A working girl who excels at doing a man's job, Nancy has none of the restrictions, conflicts, or doubts that come with a dynamic, committed life. In a world where everything, including perfection, is possible, Nancy thrives in a whirlwind of society dances, luxury travel, fraternity parties, and terrifying encounters with the scummiest of thugs. Nancy herself is full of dichotomies. A feminist who's ruled by conventional propriety, she's assertive but reasonable, self-centered but altruistic, purposeful and respectful.

Maybe it's because she didn't have a mother to hold her back, maybe it's because she's a born overachiever, or maybe it's because she likes the company of adults more than kids her own age, but Nancy's not impressed or intimidated by grown-ups. It never occurs to her that adults might have an upper hand. She chases after them with no regard for her own vulnerabilities. She grills adults relentlessly, feeling no awkwardness at being a kid. Nancy Drew—obsessed truth-seeker and straight-shooter who's smarter than most grown-ups around her—exudes authority. And that's what makes her magical, an irresistible character for young readers.

Nancy's more mature and complicated than the Hardy Boys, who hold on to their readers'

short attention spans because, like nineteenth-century frontiersmen, they are ever on the alert for danger. The Hardy Boys are always on the lookout, ready to protect their family, friends, and hometown of Bayport from whatever threatens their way of life. What a huge responsibility, what a piece of luck, what a kick for these two boys. Every cliff-hanging chapter presents Frank and Joe with excitement and another chance to show off in a world where men prove their manhood by measuring themselves against other men, over and over and over again.

Frank and Joe thrive as heroic characters for boys because they continually live on the edge. They throw powerful punches when they have to, make the most of their common sense, have access to the newest technological toys of their trade, pat each other on the back, and, because they lead a life of obsessive action, have no need to reflect on their emotions. They simply affirm their loyalties, believe in their own invulnerability and unwavering moral strength, and act out their version of masculinity in a timeless, endless loop of thrilling excitements. The Hardy Boys never stop and, like most men who are married to their jobs, can't imagine retiring.

On the other hand, unlike Frank and Joe Hardy, who join the line in the literary pantheon of male adventurers, Nancy Drew bears a special responsibility: she stakes out new territory by showing girls how to take action, how to set their sights beyond what convention expects of them. Nancy was, and remains, an original in kids' literature; she still teaches girls that it's OK to be smarter than anyone else around, that success is the appropriate reward for being an independent, curious risk-taker who knows when to persevere and when to ask for help. Nancy, always open to life's mysteries, invites her readers to seek nothing less for themselves.

The yin and yang of juvenile detectives, Nancy Drew and the Hardy Boys are alike in some important ways and opposite in others. It's a given that they're dedicated to fighting crime, doing good, and being responsible, civil citizens. But when they were created in the late twenties and their characters took shape—good boys and a good girl—for all their spirited independence, the teen sleuths had to reflect what society assumed and expected of boys and girls. The boys are fun-loving; Nancy's a more serious girl. She's emotional; Frank and Joe have no time for such sissy stuff. The three teen sleuths are equally smart, but the Hardys, because they're boys, are goal-oriented and punch their way through plots, while Nancy moves purposefully from one clue to the next, excited by every intuitive step of the process.

Fictional beacons of light in the darkness of teenage turmoil, Frank and Joe Hardy and Nancy Drew are inspirational characters who have influenced four generations of young teens, for whom the unstable, shifting ground of adolescence makes walking a straight line nearly impossible. Frank and Joe and Nancy face life head-on. Frozen in time as teenagers, their identities are firmly locked in place; their courses clear. What they do is more important than how they feel. What they fear they conquer; whatever is in their way is overcome. And because crime and evil are always with us, the three teen detectives teach kids life's most important lessons: how to have the courage to face the problems life serves up regularly, and to believe that life is worth living in a world that is worth protecting. For embedded in every one of the Hardy Boys' and Nancy Drew's relentlessly optimistic stories is a can-do, how-to message that encourages teens to persevere, reminding them that just as good triumphs over evil, youth triumphs over age.

boomerang. But Joe, watching, saw somethin
crowd did not notice. With a quick movemer
salesr and he ed tow case.
whipped it open and in one deft motion took
eal boomerang; one that if used wrongly cou

Action, Action, Action

The sun is shining, as usual, in River Heights, Nancy Drew's hometown. Flowers bloom, birds twitter, and the swell smell of fresh-baked cakes floats in the air. Maybe River Heights is the Utopia that Americans have long searched for, Eden on the banks of the Muskoka River. No one smokes, drinks, or jaywalks. Auto mechanics tell the truth. River Heights is a thriving small city somewhere in the Midwest, populated by fair-minded, generous, and polite folk.

Hundreds of miles away, just off the Atlantic coast and nestled on the edge of Barmet Bay, is picturesque Bayport. That's the little town where Frank and Joe Hardy act out their adventures, where the darkest forces of nature provide an ever-changing backdrop for excitement. It's a quaint place, edged with sunny beaches and dense dark forests, sitting atop sheer two-hundred-foot-high cliffs that are punctuated by labyrinthine caves, abandoned mines, and dank, snaking tunnels. Bayport is constantly pelted by rain, snow, sleet, and hail, and the skies are regularly electrified by lightning bolts. This is the home of 50,000 diehard optimists and good sports.

Every fictional detective gets an atmospheric, mysterious world to play in, a landscape that changes yet always stays the same. Sherlock Holmes has foggy London, and Charlie Chan can sail home to Honolulu to rest up before boarding the next clipper to New York, Paris, or Rio. Decades before Walt Disney opened the gates to

Disneyland, Edward Stratemeyer fashioned the theme-park worlds of River Heights and Bayport, where evil bubbles just below the surface and dangerous strangers peep in windows, where threats to the status quo constantly crack the veneer of small-town peace, quiet, and civility. In both communities, dastardly deeds are so carefully orchestrated and relentlessly scheduled that there's little time left for boredom. Kids who read Nancy Drew and Hardy Boys books gladly leave their own mundane worlds behind to explore these two strangely familiar bell-jar environments at Frank, Joe, and Nancy's sides, to sign on as silent sidekicks in the carefully scripted action.

River Heights and Bayport are both bordered by family farms, lakeside camps, lush golf courses, and sylvan countryside. Each lies next to a body of water, which is as ever-changing, yet familiar, as the plots in each mystery. There's a good side of town and a bad side. Streets are named after numbers, flowers, pleasant views, and sturdy trees. Both have bustling Main Streets lined with hotels and less glamorous boardinghouses, a bank, a courthouse, a library, an art museum or two, a movie theater, and a historical society. River Heights and Bayport have four newspapers apiece that routinely cover the exploits of their local supersleuths. Planes of all sizes fly in and out of the two towns' busy airports. River Heights has its Bon Ton nightclub; in Bayport, the Hardy Boys' gang hangs out at the Bon Ton confectionery. The real world stops at the edges of both towns, where no citizens suffer from the Great Depression, are called to fight in any war, or have reason to protest social injustice.

Where, exactly, are these two towns? Some Hardy Boys fans swear that Bayport is just miles away from New York City in tony Westchester

County, but others pull out maps and compasses to investigate the contradictory clues sprinkled throughout the mysteries and suggest that Bayport is down the coast in New Jersey, Delaware, Maryland, or North Carolina—or up north in Massachusetts or on the craggy coast of Maine. River Heights, though quite a bit larger than Bayport, is no easier to find. Mildred Wirt admits that when she described the small city's spirit, she put a lot of Iowa in it, and that later on when she moved to Ohio, River Heights might have moved east, too. One ace investigator, balancing text references, geology, historical events, and the psychology of the unconscious, located River Heights in east-central Ohio, south of Cleveland. But if it's there, then how do Nancy and friends hop on trains for a quick ride into Manhattan? Is Nancy's hometown in New Jersey? Truth be told, it makes no difference. Bayport and River Heights exist in the only place that matters—the imagination of the boys and girls who love to read. Leslie McFarlane, who knew the Hardy Boys' deepest secrets, had the right advice: "Don't bother to look it up. You won't find it on the map."

Even if the exact location is pure fiction, the atmosphere of each locale is palpable. The gloomy and decaying mansions in River Heights drip spiderwebs; its castles and manor houses, crowned with attics, turrets, and crenellated towers, are crammed with secret chambers, hidden staircases, and locked closets. Thriving on the intensity of sinister scariness that would terrify a lesser girl, Nancy might travel out of town for business or vacation, but she knows there's no place like home.

The Hardy Boys spend more time out of doors than Nancy does, and it's the fearsome and dynamic power of nature that permeates the atmosphere that they breathe. The unpredictable forces of nature constantly challenge Frank and Joe. Telltale tracks reveal animals on the prowl; winds howl through dark forests. The boys are at their best when blanketed by blizzards, trying to stand tall in the blast of a hurricane, or trapped in a storm, as in *Hunting for Hidden Gold* (1928):

> *The snow flung itself upon them and the wind shrieked with renewed fury as they left the unsheltered pit and entered the half-darkness of the cave mouth. It was as though they were entering a new world. They had become so accustomed to the roaring of the gale and the sweep of the storm that the interior of the passage seemed strangely peaceful and still.*

Mud slides, avalanches, primordial fires, and treacherous sandstorms never stop Frank and Joe. They get blinded by treacherous fog, spin in whirlpools on Barmet Bay, and are trapped in scary places—cul-de-sacs, caves, chasms, and on mountaintops. The Hardy Boys are always testing their teen invincibility and budding manhood as they face off against the wilderness, determined to win one more fight against death and thumb their noses at Mother Nature.

Lousy weather and rugged topography don't stop them nor does the arkful of animals that chase them over the course of the series—mountain lions, foxes, tigers, rats, grizzly bears, cougars, bulls, coyotes, wildcats, pumas, wild boars, and even a howling attack monkey. In *Hunting for Hidden Gold,* Frank and Joe, trapped in a claustrophobic underground gold mine, fight off sharp-fanged, snarling wolves:

> *Suddenly Frank thought of the revolver they had seized from Slim Briggs. It was still in his pocket and he had forgotten all about it until this time. . . . Slowly, he withdrew it. Then, turning the flashlight directly on one of the snarling beasts, he took aim and fired.*
>
> *The animal dropped in his tracks with a yelp of pain, and instantly the ranks of the wolves were broken as they fled howling to the darkest corners of the cavern. . . . Again they were trapped. Frank fired at the animal. The shot went wide and the brute slunk back, but still remained in the passageway. Two or three of the other animals came rushing out of the darkness and pounced on the body of the dead wolf, tearing at the flesh with savage jaws. For a while, the cave echoed with growls and snarls as the animals set about their hideous meal, and then the revolver crashed forth again and another wolf toppled over dead.*

Crash! Bang! Boom! Forty years before special effects came to drive the plots of action movies, the Hardy Boys faced fireballs, dynamite, and time bombs in grandfather clocks as well as in their car. Suitcase bombs, firebombs, atom crackers, and rocket blasts that heat up the skies have all propelled the action forward. They face more subtle weaponry as well: in *A Figure in Hiding* (1937), for instance, they are temporarily blinded when Dr. Grafton snaps the trigger of a gun:

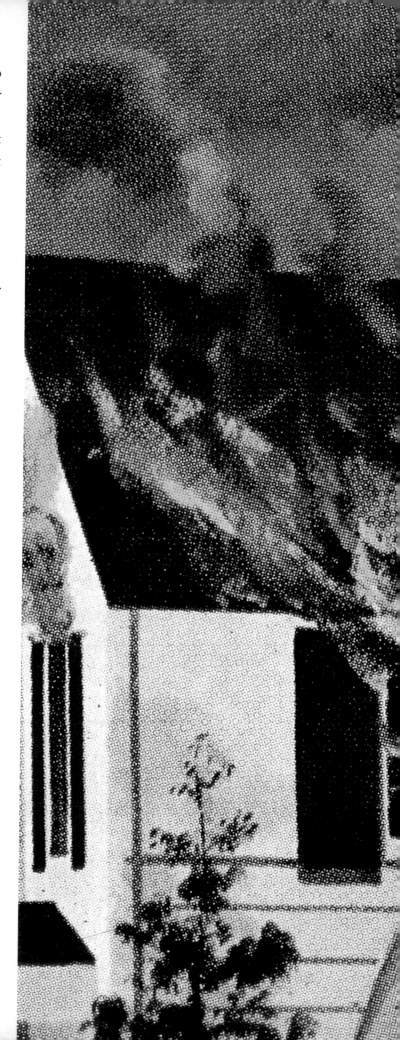

But there was no spurt of flame, no loud report! Instead, a thin stream of pungent liquid shot from the nozzle of the weapon. The next moment, Joe was gasping and choking for breath. His nostrils tingled and tears filled his smarting eyes. A strong odor of ammonia filled the air. Frank got a whiff of the vapor, and he too began to cough and gag. The boys struggled for breath, fell back, almost blinded by the irritating gas.

In their boy's version of a man's world, the Hardy Boys are not the kind of guys who sit still and watch the sun set. Like many of their young readers, who like short chapters and lots of action, they've got brief attention spans. Frank and Joe are programmed to be restless and fidgety. They're excitable, jumpy, and normal, kids who nervously tap their feet or jiggle their legs under the dinner table. When Bayport High breaks for Christmas, don't expect the Hardy Boys to stay home and trim the tree. Electrified with curiosity and eternally compelled to action, Frank and Joe are destined to travel like Odysseus, yet they share the same mythological energy and fate as Sisyphus—once they come out on top at the end of each book, they are fated to go back to ground zero in the next tale and do what they do all over again.

Unlike boys who go out looking for trouble, the Hardy Boys are blessed, because trouble's always knocking at their massive oak front door. Or, as in *The Clue of the Broken Blade* (1942), it walks right in:

"I have reason to believe that one of the biggest groups in crime is operating under our very noses," he burst forth.

"You mean right here in Bayport, Dad?" Joe exclaimed.

THE MYSTERY *of* MYSTERIES

Whether searching for *The Clue in the Embers* (1955) or climbing up *The Hidden Staircase* (1930), the Hardy Boys and Nancy Drew whet kids' appetites for detective fiction, a genre that began with the 1841 publication of Edgar Allan Poe's short story "The Murders in the Rue Morgue." In creating the first fictional detective, the eccentric and brilliant C. Augustine Dupin, Poe set up a plot formula that's been successful ever since, give or take a few shifting variables. Dupin's extraordinary reasoning powers open locked rooms, decipher the meaning of coded

The December 1943 issue of this monthly pulp was crammed with mug shots of criminals and victims, as well as stories from the police blotter, such as "Blood Bath on the Bridge to Love" and "I Spieled for Spoils in the Auction Racket."

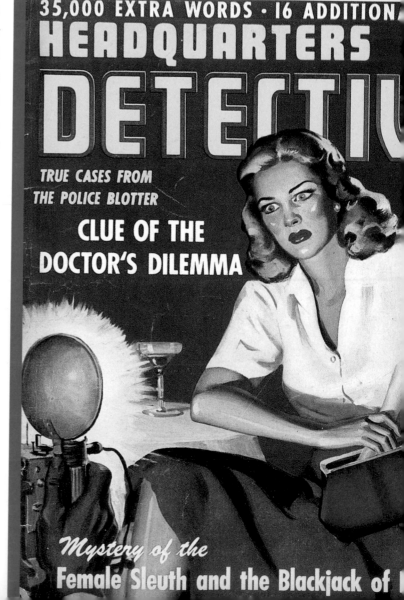

35,000 EXTRA WORDS · 16 ADDITION

HEADQUARTERS

DETECTIV

TRUE CASES FROM
THE POLICE BLOTTER

**CLUE OF THE
DOCTOR'S DILEMMA**

Mystery of the
Female Sleuth and the Blackjack of

letters, and bring hidden evidence to light. Accumulating ballistic evidence and confessions gained through psychological shock tactics reveal the least likely suspect to be the perpetrator. Poe's impartial investigator follows clues to a truth that untrained bystanders couldn't see. Replete with false leads, early detective stories tended to follow an investigating protagonist from the first scene to the last, making the unraveling a practical rather than emotional matter, a gratifying read that was also an intellectual jigsaw puzzle for its audience to solve.

Detective fiction reached the masses in 1887, when Sir Arthur Conan Doyle's Sherlock Holmes cracked *A Study in Scarlet*. Armed with his staunch skepticism, magnifying glass, pipe, and the help of his perfect foil, Dr. John Watson, Holmes captured criminals through his unfailing ability to see through the thickest smoke screens faster than Scotland Yard could. Partially due to Holmes's influence, detective fiction gained enormous popularity, and short mystery stories gave way to longer mystery novels.

The 1920s saw the appearance of Agatha Christie's Hercule Poirot, Dorothy L. Sayers's Lord Peter Wimsey, and S. S. Van Dine's Philo Vance, and the golden age of detective fiction began with high-class amateur detectives sniffing out murderers lurking in rose gardens, down country lanes, and in picturesque villages. Many conventions of the detective-fiction genre evolved in this era, as numerous writers—from populist entertainers to respected poets—tried their hands at mystery stories.

A new kind of detective novel was in the brew, too, one whose plot relied less on the snooping and sniffing of highbrow tea-drinkers and reflected a darker side of the American consciousness. By the late 1920s, Al Capone and the Mob were inspiring not only fear, but piquing genuine mainstream curiosity about the American underworld. Popular pulp fiction magazines like *Black Mask* capitalized on this, as authors such as Carrol John Daly published violent stories that focused on the mayhem and injustice surrounding the criminals, not the circumstances behind the crime. Very often, no actual mystery even existed: the books simply revolved around justice being served to those who deserved harsh treatment, which was described in explicit detail.

From Mickey Spillane's Mike Hammer to Dashiell Hammett's Sam Spade, a new breed of hard-drinking tough-talkers stalked criminals through city streets, delivering morally justifiable punishment. Bullet-riddled bodies, sexpot killers, and machine-gun blowouts became the symbols of hard-boiled detective fiction, now known as "crime novels" and lambasted by some critics, who called them "really prolonged literary lynchings." Told in stark and sometimes elegant language through the unemotional eyes of new hero-detectives, these stories were an American phenomenon.

While the classic detective novel is an exercise in logic and puzzle-solving and satisfies the rational mind's need for order to prevail, the crime novel satisfies a deeper craving. Revenge constitutes the primary motive in "hard-boiled" stories, and the detectives in the crime novel are as violent and brutal as the villains. No moral tone other than "might is right" prevails. Many novelists of the hard-boiled school tried to defend the new genre, calling it "realistic" detective fiction.

Psychologists think that mystery readers are gratified by scenes of theft, violence, and murder, that readers' dark sides revel in grisly acts that confirm people's primitive nature, and that stories give vent to the twisted desires our moral conscience suppresses. As readers vicariously become one with the detective, they add up the clues to look at the worst aspects of themselves, then get to purge any guilt they might feel in confronting the barbaric side of their personalities.

Although it was appreciated by some of the world's best minds (Franklin Roosevelt and W. B. Yeats were fans), detective fiction was believed to be sexy but dangerous—corrupting man's intellect through smart smut. But readers past and present, often scorned as suspense junkies, feel pleasure when they succumb to these books. There's an "everybody wins" element at work in mysteries; readers are drawn into a game they can't lose: careful readers have the satisfaction of figuring out the mystery before it is revealed, while readers left in the dark enjoy the thrill of a surprise ending.

American boys used to sell newspapers, mow lawns, and work as soda jerks. Girls baby-sat, sewed, and worked in libraries and shops. Teens still toil in many fields, and most parents and educators assume that a part-time job teaches discipline and self-sufficiency, but a University of Michigan study conducted in the late 1980s concluded that high school students who work are less likely to graduate or go on to college.

They can't resist its call, and neither can young fans, who become as compulsively hooked on finishing book after book as the brothers are hooked on crime-busting.

The books work because preteens are looking for role models and for clues about how to get along in the world. Between the ages of eight and twelve, kids are shedding childish fantasies to study the logic and details of everyday life. For the first time, they're able to see good and bad simultaneously and to balance them in their minds. That's why kids have fun analyzing mysteries with neat beginnings, middles, and ends; they get pleasure from piecing clues together, power from reading stories about kids who outwit adult adversaries, and a sense of control from seeing order rise from chaos. Maybe that explains why kids are so willingly seduced by action stories and whodunits.

In classic plots, the Hardy Boys face danger, fight it, and win, time and again. Frank and Joe stumble into a mystery, or else have a thorny case handed over to them by their dad, Fenton Hardy, who's out of town or busily at work on another assignment. The action's often accelerated by a warning that's phoned in, mailed, or wrapped around a rock and hurled through the window of 23 Elm Street, the Hardy family's two-story, stone-clad home, which sits overlooking Barmet Bay. These messages are seldom veiled, as *The Mark on the Door* (1934) indicates:

> *To Señor Fenton Hardy, Private Detective from the United States:*
>
> *This is to warn you and your sons that you must not set foot upon Mexican soil. If you disregard this warning, there will be one penalty, and that penalty will be—Death!*

In every book an unlikely string of fortuitous coincidences eventually leads the boys deep into the heart of trouble. The questions of who, what, when, where, and why are what drive Frank and Joe through each mystery. The fun for readers comes from the unpredictability of the details that flesh out the utterly predictable plots. In formula fiction like the Hardy Boys series, the same story is told over and over again. Young readers quickly come to love the comfortable ritual. They know that there'll be a nefarious crime, scruffy villains, frantic chases, natural disasters, and the inevitable happy ending that restores peace and stability. The

details barely matter. What galvanizes kids is the guaranteed tension, the perpetual changes of scenery, and the relentless parade of colorful characters. The constancy of crime is what keeps the Hardys on their toes and makes the books, with such seductive titles as *While the Clock Ticked* (1932) and *A Figure in Hiding*, hum with activity. A central mystery runs through each of the fifty-eight carefully structured, classic stories. Plots twist and turn with snarly subplots and enough amnesiacs, weird hermits, ventriloquists, sneaky salesmen, crazed geniuses, and pirates to guarantee that Frank's and Joe's lives will provide frantic fun for the reader.

The seaside metropolis of Bayport is an idyllic magnet for the dastardly villains who swarm through its banks, post offices, and derelict mansions like maggots on a corpse. In *The Secret of the Old Mill* (1927), Docker and a dastardly gang print the counterfeit bills that keep circulating in and around town. A gang of bank robbers comes to Bayport to kidnap Frank and Joe but mistakenly abducts their friends Chet Morton and Biff Hooper in *The Missing Chums* (1928). Criminal scum steal cars, priceless stamp collections, atomic-weapons isotopes, gold-mine leases, rare moths, and even Topnotch, the famous race horse, in *The Sinister Signpost* (1936). Evil intruders penetrate the Hardy home with such regularity that in *The Mystery of the Flying Express* (1941), Frank and Joe connect the house locks to radios that will blast loud sounds the instant that any door is jimmied. In *The Mystery of the Chinese Junk* (1960) they rip out the old burglar alarm and install an Electric Eye Snooperscope that rings bells and floods the grounds with bright light when intruders skulk. Clever bunko artists cheat unsuspecting victims, industrial spies and saboteurs plot against businesses, poachers steal livestock. Counterfeiters mock the government; cults flourish. Many criminals

work solo, but just as often they band together in gangs: in *The Flickering Torch Mystery* (1943), the Flickering Torch Gang steals construction materials from state and federal projects, while in *The Twisted Claw* (1939), the Barracuda Gang and the Twisted Claw Gang smuggle rare museum artifacts. The Olympic Health Club Gang runs an identity-changing operation for criminals in *The Masked Monkey* (1972).

No one and no place eludes crime's reach. In *A Figure in Hiding*, phony Dr. Grafton's Eye Syndicate bilks blurry-eyed oldsters with promises of restored vision. The caves perforating the coast of Barmet Bay are piled high with diamonds and illicit drugs smuggled in by crooks. They're also where the Hardy Boys find the stolen cars that solved *The Shore Road Mystery* (1928), and where they searched for the eccentric college professor Todham Todd in *The Secret of the Caves* (1929). When the action takes place in Bayport, the boys are often drawn to the waterfront, where a hodgepodge of ruffians, vendors, and beggars make Tomato Can Alley their headquarters. The district is graphically described in *The Mystery of the Flying Express* (1941) as

> [A] picturesque, but squalid part of the city. The streets were dark and crooked, crowded with second-hand stores, cheap restaurants, and cheap hotels. There was an unpleasant odor of strong food in the air. Mahogany-tanned men in caps and pea jackets strode the streets, ambling along with the rolling gait peculiar to sailors.

It's on the waterfront in the 1959 edition of *The House on the Cliff* that the boys glean whispered tips from backstreet characters like Pretzel Pete, the man with the folded ear, or the burly,

TEENS IN HARD TIMES

The Depression skewed many teens' attitudes toward jobs, money, and security for life. The poorest competed for jobs, and many left home. Some 250,000 were forced into lives of danger—riding the rails, hitchhiking from town to town, eking out money however they could to stay alive.

Prosperity couldn't mask teens' cold war anxieties. Bomb shelters stocked with canned foods and cots made a few feel secure, but for most teens in the 1950s and 1960s, the death threat of nuclear war compounded the turbulence of their adolescence.

After student deferments from the draft were abolished in 1971, many potential draftees tried to avoid going to Vietnam by feigning illness, becoming conscientious objectors, or joining the "Hell no, we won't go!" protest movement. Some fled the country or burned their draft cards.

tattooed Blackbeard whose path they cross in *The Melted Coins* (1944).

Frank and Joe are so attuned to crime's signals that they can walk down a street and overhear criminals plotting. With laserlike precision, they observe suspicious behavior and discover the clues—like twisted claws, sinister signposts, or broken blades—that start their adrenaline pumping. The boys are known for their ability to make instant decisions and act swiftly, and once they beam in on a criminal, they're tenacious and always prepared. The Hardy Boys' pockets bulge with tools of their trade: flashlights, pocket knives, waterproof matches, stout cord, skeleton keys, worthless papers to swap for valuable documents, handkerchiefs, miniature shortwave radios, magnets, fingerprint powder, and, for when they lose their bearings, compasses.

In the fingerprinting lab and photographic developing room in their cellar and in their laboratory over the garage, the boys practice the techniques that made their father successful.

"Hey, Dad!" Joe exclaimed. "Think we might get anything from this?"

Fenton Hardy squatted down to examine the paper remnant. "It's worth a try.". . . The charred paper was gently swept onto a glass plate, then sprayed with fixative, and flattened under another plate. Later, in the boys' crime lab at home, the scrap was photographed on an orthochromatic plate and printed on high-contrast paper. Three words could be made out in the ghostly scrawl: Aardvark to Canada.

The Short-Wave Mystery *(1966)*

The boys also use Fenton Hardy's extensive crime library to help crack secret codes and dig deep into the records of previous criminal cases.

Mr. Hardy, a master of disguises known for using makeup, masks, wigs, and costumes to conceal his well-known identity, has handed down this bag of tricks to his sons, as well. In the 1962 edition of *The Missing Chums,* Frank and Joe smudge their faces and artfully rip their clothes to pass for beachcombers. In other books they masquerade as gorillas, messengers, fishermen, construction workers, magicians, and skid-row kids. In *The Disappearing Floor* (1940), big and little brother even dress up in gowns and wigs and pass themselves off as Cynthia and Jeannie—two old ladies.

Their brains, brawn, and crime-busting skills would be worthless, though, if Frank and Joe had to depend on Bayport's buses and taxicabs to track fiends around town and to nearby Great Notch, Cherryville, Willowville, Beach Grove, or Doeville. They ride matching motorcycles in their very first book, *The Tower Treasure,* and their

circle of action widened when they bought their first car, a roadster painted nickel color, with the reward money they received for solving *The Shore Road Mystery.* It is only the first of many autos that the brothers would own: they drive a yellow convertible in *While the Clock Ticked,* a sporty green coupe in *The Sign of the Crooked Arrow* (1949), and another convertible in *The Ghost at Skeleton Rock* (1957). The *Sleuth,* a trim motorboat, enables them to chase offshore criminals in, among other adventures, *The Secret of the Old Mill* (1927). Whether on land or water, speed's of the essence, and the boys barely blink an eye when their motorcycles fly off the road, the *Sleuth* is menaced by swells or crooks, or their cars skid, spin, and tilt up on two wheels. They're as cool as crash-test dummies.

Frank and Joe don't whine, they don't scream, they don't cry. Nor do their brave hearts skip a beat when the plane they're coasting in suddenly

THE *nuclear* FAMILY *explodes*

The Loud family became stars for all the wrong reasons in the 1973 public television series *An American Family.*

In 1973, when Americans were tuning in to *The Waltons* and *Little House on the Prairie*, *An American Family* promised a televised peep into the contemporary dream family—a *real* family. The stars of the twelve-hour public television documentary, the five Loud children and their parents, were chosen for their sunny good looks, ranch-style house, swimming pool, and two-car lifestyle. The Louds' life was revealed to America in one-hour, weekly installments, and it wasn't always pretty: Americans watched as Bill and Pat's twenty-year marriage fell apart, the family's eldest son came out as a homosexual, and the four other children suffered from a sense of aimlessness. As families watched in fascination and slowly absorbed the sad truth of the Loud story, the unspoken problems in their own homes became a more tangible reality.

The myth of the ideal nuclear family has taken a toll on Americans' consciences over the last three decades as they struggled to live up to a symbol of stability glorified more through nostalgic remembrance than supported by fact. During the Depression, economic instability and limited housing options helped to foster a group mentality in a country that often valued individualism above all else. And as the country pulled together out of necessity, so did families. Many households expanded to include multiple generations and diverse relations, all drawing on one another for economic, emotional, and recreational sustenance.

But economic hardships took their toll. Men, ashamed of their inability to provide, sometimes turned abusive, and women, struggling to make ends meet, became overworked.

Families in the fifties lived in an era of unprecedented prosperity, and many adults who had grown up with the deprivation of the Depression and the sacrifice and threat of World War II now poured their energies into providing stable and comfortable environments for their families. Victory in the war affirmed for many Americans the sanctity of their institutions, and no institutions were more important than marriage and the family. Men and women were encouraged to center their identities around the family, which became a shield from the realities of the outside world. Divorce and illegitimacy rates fell under this pressure, but at the same time, people refused to acknowledge that as the economy grew, sharp gender divides were forcing many women to stay at home, while the pressure to succeed brought drinking among men (and women) to a new high.

But Americans choose not to remember this flip side. Instead, they recall the bright new world they created, full of intact, apparently happy families. This world was destined to crumble, though, under the powerful political and social movements of successive decades, a victim of its own prosperity. With the hippie movement and student demonstrations of the sixties came the notion that authority could, and should, be questioned, that institutions were perhaps not so sacrosanct. Formerly oppressed groups—women, gays, ethnic minorities—agitated for, and often won, rights that they had been denied. But as individuals pursued their interests, the family took a beating: divorce rates exceeded one million per year by the mid-1970s, and the strength of the American family was left shaky at best. In the face of such rapid change, the past is idealized, and its already impossible standard further raised.

Around the turn of the century, before there were child-labor laws, 1.75 million children worked to help their families survive. By the prosperous 1950s, many kids were living on easy street, responsible for only the few odd household tasks that new labor-saving appliances couldn't accomplish. Chores became symbolic, a way to teach responsibility, discipline, and teamwork. For their work at home, many teens earned allowances and got their first on-the-job training in capitalism. Today only a small percentage of kids take out the trash, mow the lawn, and vacuum. When they do, studies show that most girls cooperate because they want to help the family out, while boys are motivated by the cash.

nose-dives. In *What Happened at Midnight* (1931), Frank and Joe are quick to act when the pilot tells them to get out on the wing if they hope to save themselves:

> [They] clung for a moment; glanced back at the pilot . . . "Jump!"
>
> Twisting and turning through the air, the lads plunged toward the earth. Desperately Frank groped for the ring of the rip cord. It eluded his grasp. Sudden panic gripped him . . . he was dropping toward earth at ever-increasing speed. He might already have reached an altitude too low to permit the parachute to open in time. Then his groping hand found the ring. He gripped it convulsively and tugged at it.
>
> Nothing happened . . .

Despite the perpetual threats to life and limb, the Hardys always come out alive and continue to roll with the punches, battling ghosts, chasing sleepwalkers, exhuming mummies, dodging psychopaths, and eluding the grip of creeps who threaten to tattoo them. Heads get bashed, jaws punched, and teeth rattled as the boys rely on quick reflexes and fancy footwork to defend themselves.

When trouble strikes, it usually hits accident-prone Joe first. He's the one who'll get knocked out flat by a fire truck or fall from a second-story hotel window through a glass canopy. In *The Secret Warning* (1938), he is blown sky-high when a dry cleaner explodes and later nearly has the life squeezed out of him by a slimy giant octopus. It's Frank who saves him, every time.

One close shave follows another, keeping kids reading and rooting for the Hardys. There's no room for sulky boys in a Hardy Boys world: though no one ever gets killed in a Hardy Boys story, or any Stratemeyer Syndicate book, mayhem and menace keep the brothers in constant jeopardy.

The 212 pages of breathless action that comprise *The Secret of Wildcat Swamp* (1952) are a good example, as Frank and Joe skirt peril and death thirty-four times. Things go wrong from the

LEAVE TOWN
AT ONCE OR
THERE'LL BE
TROUBLE

start; *Skyhappy Sal,* the plane that's taking them and their science teacher, Cap Bailey, out west to track down rare fossils, careens out of control upon takeoff. From there, trouble hits in waves.

Once they're in the wide-open plains, the boys face robbers, who lock them in a train's refrigerator car, from which they escape up to the roof just as the train goes through a low tunnel. No sooner do they jump off than the speeding train crashes off an embankment. Not much later, Frank and Joe are hiding in the back of a huge tractor-trailer truck carrying huge, heavy iron pipes, and are nearly crushed to death when the contents shift. They're forced to jump out to the ground, where nature is no kinder. Wildcats lurk. The brothers nearly step on poisonous snakes, boulders crash around them, fires rage, and Joe sinks in quicksand. In the Old West, where bullets fly, the boys are pursued by phony rangers who ambush them, kidnap them, and hit, bind, and gag them. They're thrown across saddles, imprisoned in corrals, and the book climaxes with the boys scaling a rickety mountaintop tower that explodes.

Cliff-hangers routinely end each of the books' chapters. In *The Disappearing Floor* (1940), chapter three, "A Desperate Plunge," ends ominously: "It's too late. With a splintering crash, the car burst through the drawbridge gate and hurled itself into space."

So does chapter five, "A Cry for Help": "'Look out!' roared a man in the crowd. 'He's going to shoot!' The excited mob ducked; that is, all but one person. This fellow delivered a crushing blow to Frank's head. It sent the lad spinning into the gutter."

And so does chapter six, "Frank's Plan," which brings the kids to another brink:

"Get back!" he whispered in desperation. "Somebody else is coming." Joe's face blanched with horror as the figure of a native of India, in the full garb of a

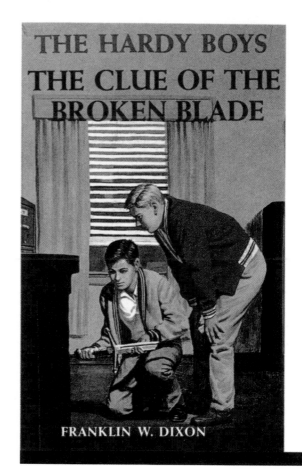

prince, stepped noiselessly through the entrance to the cave. A pair of cruel-looking eyes blinked in the rays of the two flashlights on the ground.

And chapter twenty-one, "The Deadly Switchboard," ends with Mr. Hardy in danger:

"Better stand back, boys," said their father grimly. He put on a pair of insulated gloves and stretched his hand toward the knob. At the instant his fingers closed over the object there was a brilliant flash and a loud crackle. The detective crumpled.

"The gloves didn't work," groaned Joe, bending over his father.

Most of the time, the Hardy Boys have only themselves to count on in such predicaments. Every now and then their friends help out, but Frank and Joe have learned from experience that they can't count on the Bayport police.

Chief of Police Collig is a fat, pompous official who has never been blessed by an overabundance of brains. His chief satellite and aide-de-camp is Oscar Smuff, a detective on the Bayport police force. As the Hardys' friend Chet Morton remarks in *The Short-Wave Mystery* (1945), "If you bother to put their brains together you'd have enough for a half-wit!"

Frank and Joe's other contact on the force is little better. He's described, somewhat unkindly, in *The Phantom Freighter* (1947):

> *Con Riley, who was on the Bayport police force, was slow-witted and never given any very important work to do. . . . The policeman was wary of the Hardys, for they usually outguessed him, and a few times unwittingly had made him the laughingstock of the other policemen.*

But even in the midst of tumult, the Hardy Boys always remain polite young gentlemen, respecting the Stratemeyer Syndicate's implicit code of morality. Frank and Joe and their pals may get knocked around or razzed by all sorts of unsophisticated hayseeds, such as the Crabb Corner Gang in *What Happened at Midnight* (1931), but they don't come to blows or lose their composure. "Gosh" or "golly" is the fiercest expletive that will pass the Hardy Boys' lips.

With these model-citizen characters routinely in peril, all the reader needs to do to save them is to turn the page, and the Hardy Boys are back on their feet. But being smart, and tough when they need to be, isn't always enough to save them, and they fall right back into the enemy's clutches and have to throw a few more punches in one last clash before the bad guys are trounced and loose ends get tied up. Then Frank and Joe collect kudos from Dad, the cops—even the most obtuse and comic ones like Chief Collig and Detective Smuff—who reluctantly acknowledge their skills, and the people they've helped. The boys also

THE *shook-up* GENERATION

The threat of an estimated one million juvenile delinquents so terrorized Americans that in 1955 President Eisenhower asked for a budget increase of $3 million to combat the teen scourge.

Rebellion—from class-cutting to drug experimentation—is one way teenagers grow into themselves, breaking rules contrived by someone else and setting new ones. But the threat of something bigger than mere rule-breaking—juvenile delinquency—began unnerving parents and making headlines (or was it vice versa?) in the 1930s. Two-thirds of American teenagers were spending their days in high school, away from the watchful eyes of parents. Looking to each other for role models, they developed a new teen culture replete with forbidden allure—the charms of swing music, the hope of romance, and activities, such as sex and drinking, usually restricted to adults. Saddle shoes, slang, celebrity fan clubs, and thigh-flashing jitterbug dances alienated parents, who worried that their teens were growing up too fast.

During World War II, "victory girls," or "V-girls," began exchanging sexual favors for presents from soldiers, and soon the rise in venereal diseases among fighting-age men demanded national attention. Then, when white soldiers stationed in California began dating young Mexican American women, they angered many *pachucos,* or Mexican American teenagers, and helped fuel the "zoot suit" riots of 1943. Fanning the flames were books and movies depicting sensational brutality in teen lives; these frequently opened by citing FBI Director J. Edgar Hoover's 1942 report of a 21 percent increase in juvenile crime, 40 percent increase in

drunkenness among girls under twenty-one, and 64 percent increase of teenage prostitution. Hysteria swept over the country, abetted by Hoover, who in 1943 warned that "A creeping rot of moral disintegration is eating into our nation."

Responding to the "threat," in the first six months of 1943, magazines published twelve hundred articles on juvenile delinquency, including "Are These Our Children?," which told of teen problems that had formerly been written off as working-class antics—drinking, smoking reefer, vandalism, and promiscuity—emerging among mainstream, or middle-class, teens. Fearful state officials in the Midwest tried to outlaw jukeboxes; expert witnesses testifying at congressional hearings advocated the construction of "teen towns" where teens could go to dance, drink sodas, and safely exercise their desires for independence.

Postwar Hollywood producers, eager to capitalize on teens' new spending power, released movies like *Youth Runs Wild* and *Live Fast, Die Young,* stories of fast cars, sex-crazed girls, and tragic deaths that put a chill into the hearts of fearful parents. In the 1954 movie *The Wild One,* Marlon Brando donned the tight jeans and leather jacket worn by lower-class boys and made them sexy for everyone. Elvis Presley, with his swiveling pelvis and "negro sound," became an idol to teens, and when James Dean crashed his speeding Porsche just before the 1955 release of *Rebel Without a Cause,* he became their tragic hero. Parents worrying about their kids' morals, safety, and futures were at the end of their ropes.

But what looked like deviance to some actually helped teens define themselves as a group—by dressing and acting a new part, listening to "their" music, and using "their" words. And teen rule-breaking wasn't *all* bad: it would have significant national and worldwide impact in the civil rights movement and opposition to U.S. actions in Vietnam.

collect substantial rewards. Over the years, they bank thousands of Depression dollars, are awarded stock shares in a blue-amber mine, receive a gift certificate from the Bayport travel agency for a "fine" vacation whenever they can make it, receive a new motion-picture camera, a gold watch, and, in *The Crisscross Shadow* (1953), a round of applause and a big circle of gifts from the Ramapan Indians for helping to locate a land deed and a jeweled dagger. Their wealth even trickles down to Laura Hardy, who cashes in Prince Dharmuk's handsome gift of a ruby ring honoring "the mother of two of the bravest boys he's ever known" in *The Hooded Hawk Mystery* (1954).

If the Hardy Boys thrive on a steady diet of thrills, Nancy Drew is defined by the challenge and success that crime-busting brings her. Nancy has no mother to apprentice herself to, no homework that needs to be done. She has no worry about money nor chores to do around the house. But shopping at Burk's Department Store or eating dainty luncheons with her nice but conventional friends just isn't enough for ambitious Nancy Drew. The only time she feels truly alive is when she's on a job, and no sooner is one case solved than the junior career gal worries, "Will I ever again be so excited?" When Nancy's not working she feels "empty"; she can't sit still and seems listless at play. Lucky for her that just as she's obsessively thinking that she'd "go to the ends of the earth to find another mystery," someone in need rings her doorbell, or something unsettling—like a stolen rosebush or a ghost sighting—grabs her attention and snaps her back to life.

Nancy's eager to serve the broken, hapless victims of the world—sickly old ladies who have been swindled out of property and inheritances, first-generation immigrant inventors at a loss when they're robbed of their patents, sweet

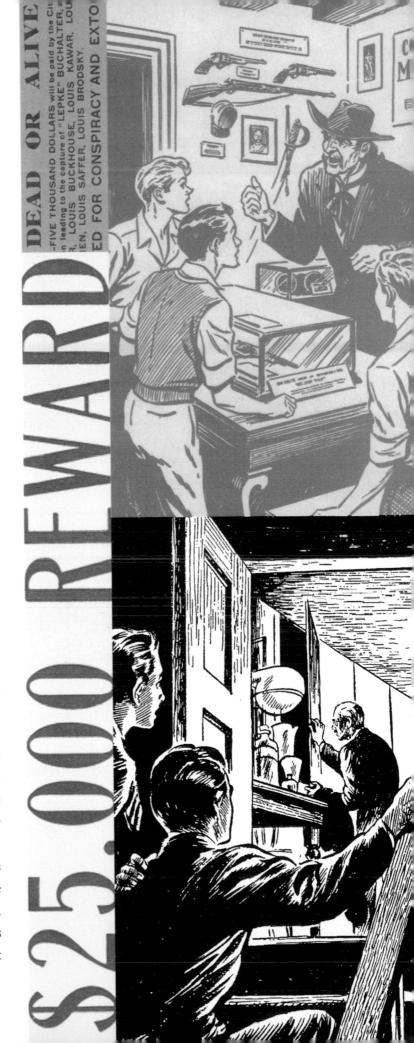

orphans and wards doomed to financial and emotional abuse at the hands of mean and greedy guardians. She's a savior to down-on-their-luck types, people who've seen better days and who'll face ruin unless Nancy takes up their causes. And she does, because, quite simply, it's her calling.

Nancy Drew is programmed to do good, and her mysteries follow a traditional recipe that's guaranteed to work every time. Each book balances a tangle of multiple plot lines and outrageous coincidences that move the action forward. There are false panels to tap on, mysterious stairways and secret rooms to be found, cryptic codes to be cracked. Most cases begin in the comfortable Drew home, a large, red-brick dwelling shaded by tall, beautiful trees, set far back from the street at the end of a path lined with Nancy's prizewinning flowers described in *The Password to Larkspur Lane* (1933):

> *Father and daughter strolled up and down the flagstone paths, admiring the blossoms. Phlox and painted daisies, snapdragon and calendula, petunias, and verbenas made a gay patchwork of rose and red, yellow, violets, blue—all the colors of the spectrum. At a*

In 1950, psychoanalyst Erik Erikson talked about teens feeling overwhelmed by the many choices they face and described their state of "identity diffusion." Kids can bolster their shaky identities by hanging out in cliques that share similar abilities, likes, and dislikes. In their solidarity, often under the leadership of a more charismatic member, cliques sometimes ostracize other kids, trying to make themselves feel better by making others feel worse. A 1978 study of Boston high school students described names for members of various cliques, which included *jocks, motorheads, rednecks, nerds, dweebs, freaks, airheads, douche bags, dudes, fleabags, potheads, dirt balls, band fags, wimps, war pigs, brains, punks, weirdos, acid heads, greasers, homeys, bougies,* and *rah-rahs.*

turn of the walk, they entered the beds where the perennial flowers bloomed. Towering above all the rest were the delphiniums.

Nancy's entreated by some poor victim, enlisted to assist her father or some other authority, or stumbles into a conundrum herself before she launches a tentative investigation to find something that's been stolen or to rescue someone in need. It's not uncommon for some menacing person to warn her to back off just as she's warming up, but it's always too late: once Nancy makes up her mind, there's no turning back. She'll go without sleep. She'll give up a date. In the early books, she'll even break the law to suit her needs, if that's what it takes to find the missing cash, recover the stolen will, or foil the counterfeiter.

Nancy's a well-bred girl, but that never stops her from overstepping the boundaries of decorum. She has been trained to listen attentively to

people, so they're more than willing to pass along essential information. She'll eavesdrop if they aren't—Nancy's not embarrassed to snoop. She'll trespass if she has to, and when she does, she gets away with it, because cops all around know her reputation and her dad's. They may refer to her as "Miss Know-It-All," but they're smart enough to let her work solo. With style and grace, she picks locks and harvests information from people's homes, police files, and corporate offices. She dons disguises: in *The Password to Larkspur Lane*, she gets admitted to the sanatorium as an elderly patient, and she powders her blonde hair gray and puts on a long, old dress to pass herself off as Mrs. Frisby, the cleaning woman, in *The Quest of the Missing Map* (1942).

Nancy solves her cases through a combination of skill and luck. She is alert, always taking in the details and subtleties of the world around her— the landscapes she drives though, the decor of the rooms she visits, the clothes people wear, the way food is prepared and presented. She notices torn seams, objects moved from their customary places, and the nuances of people's behavior. But in addition, clues, like the fingerprinted sheet of paper in *The Phantom of Pine Hill* (1965) and the carrier pigeon in *The Password to Larkspur Lane*, literally fall out of the sky to land at her feet or hit her on the head. Each mystery is packed with clues— mysteries within mysteries—whose meanings must be figured out: sentimental clues, such as ballet slippers and diaries bound in red leather and velvet, hold special significance, like boxes that may yield hidden answers, precious Inca gold, sapphires, or even securities. In *The Clue in the Jewel Box* (1943), an enameled Easter egg opens to reveal a tiny tree made of emeralds, a nightingale on its branch.

As intelligent as Nancy is, she sometimes becomes so obsessed with her mission that her

judgment clouds over and she gets reckless. She'll ignore warnings, chase red herrings, and take senseless risks. Time after time, she brushes off the concern of friends, experts, and sensible adults. This casual attitude toward danger leads her, and sometimes her friends, into trouble. In *The Mystery of the Moss-Covered Mansion* (1971), Nancy rejects the advice of an animal trainer who instructs her, Bess, and George to stay clear of a huge black leopard:

> *Nancy looked over her shoulder. The trainer was gone. She said eagerly, "Let's turn around and follow this side to find out what we can."*

High school is the center of most teenagers' lives, a world of study, extracurricular activities, and cafeteria smells and sounds, *above*. High school is also where most kids start to think about career paths. In the 1920s, wealthy kids who thought of going to college studied academic subjects, while poorer students took vocational-training classes to acquire the skills that would help them find jobs. In the 1940s, three-quarters of fourteen- to seventeen-year-olds attended high school. Today, the figure is over 95 percent.

"Oh, please don't!" Bess begged. "Those animals may come after us again, and the leopard might jump over the fence!"

"I'm willing to take the chance, George, are you?" Nancy asked.

Nancy's mobility keeps the plot engines running, too. Around River Heights, she's instantly recognizable in her famous blue roadster (which is often described as being yellow, and once maroon), or, later in her career, zooming around in a convertible. Always on the move, Nancy is the kind of girl whose foot hits the gas pedal as the traffic light's changing from red to green. Heads turn in envy and admiration when Nancy, exuding all the dash and confidence of a man behind the wheel, cruises by. Traffic doesn't faze her; she maneuvers into the tightest parking spots and pulls off U-turns with ease. Still, following her father's advice, Nancy is a defensive driver: she always uses directional signals and is mindful of conditions; she stays off the roads when they're slippery. Still, her car's been smashed from the side, rear-ended by trucks, and pitched headlong into water. She even drives a borrowed car into a river in *The Clue of the Whistling Bagpipes* (1964). Yet when her car gets totaled, Carson Drew never shakes a lawyer's finger in blame. He buys his Nancy a new one to keep her rolling.

As her automotive adventures prove, Nancy's world is a dangerous place. The world's on fire; houses, factories, and forests blaze. A rented plane carrying Nancy and Carson Drew collides with a pine tree and has its landing gear sheared off. Trains are wrecked; boats sink. Nancy herself is bound, gagged, choked, gassed, poisoned, abducted, trapped underground, and, in *The Mystery at Lilac Inn* (1930), left to drown:

Many adolescent milestones are personal—first shave, first period, first date, first kiss. Others, like the day you entered high school, are more public markers on the road to adulthood. The day that you can legally drive is one; in most states the age is sixteen, although eight states license fifteen-year-olds and four have no age minimum at all. For a good part of the century, American boys considered eighteen, the age at which they registered for the draft, a marker of manhood. Then came Vietnam and the cry from the streets: "If we're old enough to fight, we're old enough to vote." Voting was the official pass to the adult world. Until 1971, a person had to be twenty-one to vote, but in that year, a constitutional amendment gave eighteen-year-olds the right to vote. At least politically, they were now their parents' equals.

Nancy Drew was left to her fate. . . . When Nancy had been flung to the floor by the crash, the gag across her mouth had loosened. . . . "Help! Help!" she screamed. . . . Cold sweat broke out on Nancy's brow as she realized that there was little hope of a rescue. She could feel the boat listing. At any moment it might plunge beneath the waves. She tugged desperately at the cords which held her a prisoner, and again she raised her voice in the frantic call: "Help!" There was a long moment of silence, a moment which to Nancy Drew seemed an eternity. Then, from far away, she heard an answering shout. "Hello, there! What's the matter?"

"Save me! Save me!" Nancy screamed as loudly as she could. "I'm locked up in the cabin."

She's also locked in closets, attics, cellars, gymnasiums, cisterns, caves, and submarines. She suffers from blackouts, and she falls frequently—down staircases and elevator shafts, over mountain ledges. She's jolted by electrical shocks from a mechanical puppet (in *The Clue of the Dancing Puppet* [1962]), hurled through the air by explosives, crushed by landslides and avalanches. One conscientious Nancy Drew lover counted "more than thirty occasions on which Nancy is bludgeoned into unconsciousness by blows to the head." Time after time, she is left for dead.

Despite all the hardships and physical threats that she endures, Nancy's power over people is that she's smarter than they are and she makes no bones about knowing it. When bozos resort to clumsy, melodramatic ploys, Nancy, who abhors cowards, strikes back with the strongest weapon she has: the truth. And once the truth is uncovered, mysteries are solved in a crescendo of swift events, including one last catastrophe striking before Nancy extracts herself from harm's way or is rescued by cops, family, or friends. Crooks are rounded up, confessions spew from culprits' lips, and all lingering questions are answered as, thanks to Nancy, order reigns again.

And then, with a shy nod, a blush, and a brief

thank-you acknowledging those who have helped her, Nancy takes in praise and accepts offerings. Unlike the Hardy Boys, she won't take cash, but she'll never turn down a request to pose for newspaper photographers. She graciously accepts property in Canada in *The Message in the Hollow Oak* (1935), a rare Paul Revere bell in *The Mystery of the Tolling Bell* (1946), and Snowball, the white Angora kitten, in *The Mystery of the Brass-Bound Trunk* (1940). Other spoils of Nancy's work include an oil portrait of herself painted by Henri Fontaine and given to her by the thankful, freedom-loving citizens of Centrovia in *The Scarlet Slipper Mystery* (1954), a yellow evening dress spun of spider silk in *The Secret in the Old Attic* (1944), enough glossy mink pelts to make a lovely scarf in *The Mystery at the Ski Jump* (1952), and, in *The Clue of the Leaning Chimney* (1949), an oriental vase emblazoned with her heroic image and the Chinese words *Hsiu Lan* ("graceful orchid"). And that's only the heavy stuff: she gets enough cameos, rings, bracelets, earrings, and jewelry studded with precious stones to fill a bank safe.

Rewards for readers are equally bountiful. Ludicrously complex plots may vibrate with intrigue and make girls gasp, but the subtext of Nancy's adventures resonates long after the plot particulars are forgotten. Unlike Hardy Boys stories, which celebrate conventional and uncomplicated manly accomplishment, Nancy Drew mysteries have always imparted a radical idea to girls—that it's okay to take action, be smart, compete, talk back, fight, succeed. That message has kept Nancy popular among girls for decades. For despite all the talk about equality between males and females, girls still have to walk on eggshells when it comes to asserting themselves and finding out what independence really means.

*   *   *

teens TAKE a STAND

Fifteen-year-old Elizabeth Eckford, one of nine teenagers who in 1957 integrated the 2,000-member student body of Central High School in Little Rock, Arkansas, tries to get to class in spite of taunts from white protesters.

At a time when most teens were worrying about clothes, blemishes, or popularity, certain black teenagers in the southern states during the fifties and sixties were mobilizing to change the course of American history. Risking their lives, these young people organized sit-ins, marched in nonviolent protests, and broke through educational barriers, forcing the nation to face its racism.

In September 1957, eight Little Rock teenagers, accompanied by Daisy Bates, president of the Arkansas NAACP, were on their way to Central High School in Little Rock, Arkansas, with the intention of integrating classes. They were stopped by the National Guard, which was sent by Governor Orval Faubus to keep the students out, but they refused to return home. The standoff hardly came out of the blue: in a 1954 Supreme Court ruling, *Brown* v. *Board of Education,* Chief Justice Earl Warren had written, "Separate educational facilities are inherently unequal," and declared school segregation unconstitutional. In response, eighty-two representatives and nineteen senators from the old Confederacy announced their opposition to the Supreme Court's decision and encouraged schools to fight integration.

Elizabeth Eckford, one of the black teens, had not received word of the group's meeting place and arrived at the school alone. After pictures of her confronting the guards were broadcast on national television, President Eisenhower addressed the nation on TV, taking a firm stand for integration. He ordered the National Guard to secure the safety of the students, who entered Central High only to endure a tumultuous, terrifying year of study.

If the Little Rock Nine provided a wake-up call for many Americans, then the 1963 Children's Crusade of Birmingham, Alabama, upped the ante in the civil rights movement in America. The Rev. Martin Luther King Jr.'s decision to hold a march in Birmingham—a city known for turning a blind eye to the ravages of the Ku Klux Klan and to the rape, castration, assault, and killing of blacks—was deemed brave by some and foolish by others. On May 2, more than 1,000 black youths, ages six to sixteen, met at the Sixteenth Street Baptist Church to begin their march. They left the church in groups of fifty, walking into the waiting arms of policemen, who hauled them to jail on charges including trespassing, parading without a permit, and loitering. Six hundred arrests were made, and, after five days, 2,000 children were in jail. "Bull" Connor, Birmingham's commissioner of safety, grew angrier as the spectacle surrounding the children's actions drew more black spectators, and national attention, with each passing day. By ordering police to release German shepherds on the crowd, and commanding firemen to disperse teenage demonstrators with blasts of water from high-pressure hoses, Connor unwittingly staged a field day for the media. President Kennedy and his brother Robert, the U.S. attorney general, persuaded black and white citizens to agree to end the demonstrations, desegregate lunch counters, rest rooms, and drinking fountains in downtown department stores, and release the demonstrators from jail. But negotiations broke down, and when King's brother's house was bombed on May 11, riots broke out anew.

Before rock 'n' roll, bobby-soxers danced to swing music and swooned to Frank Sinatra's ballads. Some historians claim rock 'n' roll was born in 1951, when disk jockey Alan Freed started playing rhythm-and-blues by black artists on his nightly radio show. But none deny that by the end of the decade, teenagers made weekly pilgrimages to neighborhood record stores, department stores, and wherever 45s were sold, to spend $50 million a year on the latest rock 'n' roll hits.

As extraordinarily accomplished and self-confident as Nancy is, and as athletic and macho as the Hardy Boys are, they all need to step back and take a break from their stressful, workaholic lives once in a while. So when the action takes a U-turn away from danger, Nancy and Frank and Joe get to act like their readers' equals. When they eat hamburgers, go shopping, giggle over stupid jokes, tease their friends, and flirt with romance, it makes their superhero status a lot easier to take. In each series, too, the sleuths head a teen clique and count on their chums to be not only buddies to hang out with, but also key parts of their professional backup systems. The kids around Nancy, Frank, and Joe also help to pull readers closer, because they are more normal and less idiosyncratic than their leaders; they're more like the kids reading the books, teens with personality tics that the main characters float high above.

In Nancy's world, she's looked up to by her small circle of well-bred, privileged girlfriends who come from comfortable, if somewhat smaller, middle-class homes. They juggle girlish joys, like shopping and chatting about diets, with activities that include boating and golf. Nancy, of course, is closer to some girls than to others. When Nancy first began breaking bread with her friends, it was Helen Corning who got to sit by Nancy's side. Helen's a typical River Heights teen, an attractive party girl searching for the perfect mate, but she's a gossip with an uneven temperament and questionable moral fiber, so Nancy never gets too close to her. Soon Helen is replaced by the pair of cousins, Bess Marvin and a girl named George Fayne. They are like bookends that represent the two warring sides of adolescence—male and female, tough and soft, brash and insecure, active and passive. They'll do almost anything for Nancy because she perks up their boring lives, and she likes to have them around to help her out in times of need. They also have just enough quirks and personality to make her shine.

Bess and George become Nancy's trusted accomplices in 1931, in *The Secret of Shadow Ranch,* and together they form a trio as tight as the Three Graces. In their teen troika, each character reflects a chunk of what a real girl thinks about, feels, and does. High-strung, compassionate Bess Marvin keeps busy covering up her own insecurities. She is obsessed with boys, her looks, and bad-hair days, and in *The Mystery of the Tolling Bell* gets the girls into hot water when she spends all her money shopping for Mon Coeur cosmetics, some of which turn out to be poisonous. She's a flirt with a weight problem, a girl who eats to gather courage. When Bess reaches for her fifth chicken sandwich in *The Clue in the Diary* (1932), she has a bundle of rationalizations ready to go: "George got away with as much food as I did—only she eats so fast you don't notice how much she's devoured." Still, Bess is not a narcissist; she's a girl who laughs at herself, and, when the going gets tough, she is the first to cry. A feminine girl who takes music lessons and wears flattering dresses, Bess is the one who'll shriek at the sight of rats and spiders. If she feels scared, she's not afraid to show it.

Freckle-faced George Fayne, on the other hand, is a tomboy with a tall, slim build and a turned-up nose. Don't call her Georgia, Georgette, or any feminized version of the name she got when her parents were expecting a boy. George confidently cuts her dark hair as short as the style allows, and combs and brushes it as infrequently as possible, not giving a hoot whether people approve or not. She wears tailored clothes and not a speck of jewelry. Indifferent to boys and full of attitude, George takes cheap shots at her cousin's chubbiness, fondness for cuddly animals, and romantic attitude. A realist in a fictional world, she knows that she doesn't have what it takes to attract boys, but neither does she care. George is self-assured, athletic, and strong; she knows judo and wins first place in the local water ballet. And while she may scream "YIKES!" when she's bitten by a poisonous centipede, abducted by a large baboon, or splattered with red ink, she bounces back from these mishaps and others, like her falls into wells, water holes, and other muddy places. Nancy can count on her to be the level-headed, gutsy friend who'll stick by her side.

If Nancy's girlfriends can be somewhat reluctant when danger kicks in or the action starts to pick up, the Hardy Boys' gang's response to action is strictly Pavlovian. At the ring of a telephone or the honk of a jalopy's horn, they're out the front door. They're boys' boys training to be men, and they pass their time playfully with blindfolded boxing matches and snowball fights, or boating on Barmet Bay in their ragtag flotilla of speedboats.

Among their classmates at Bayport High are all kinds of boys—farm boys, working-class kids, brainiacs, and weight lifters. Along with a couple of girls, they make up the crowd that hangs out at Bill's Burgers, the Bon Ton, or Mike's Munchery.

The friend Frank and Joe rely on most is farm boy Chester "Chet" Morton, who is part of the action in every book. Chet's the feminine foil for the Hardy Boys; he's the worrier, the food provider, the boy who feels fear and alerts readers to danger, which Frank and Joe never seem to notice until they're hit over the head with it. A chubby, happy-go-lucky, funny kid bursting with entrepreneurial zeal, Chet's a regular boy, a prankster who laughs when he's tickled, snores when he sleeps, stammers when he's flustered, sweats when he exerts himself, and turns as red as a beet when he's embarrassed.

When Chet isn't busy making his own fudge,

he throws himself into adolescent diversions, practicing judo, fooling around with photography, or learning how to throw his voice. He's always dreaming up moneymaking schemes: Chet teaches himself taxidermy in *The Short-Wave Mystery* when he thinks it's a way to make a buck; in *The Masked Monkey,* he organizes the gang to dredge up sunken golf balls and sell them back to country club managers. In *The Phantom Freighter,* he invents a mechanical herring that he plans to sell to commercial fishermen to use as bait, because they'll last a lifetime.

Boys dream about cars—the ones they'll never have, like a new Cadillac with big fins and lots of chrome, *opposite,* and the ones they get to live with and learn to love, like an old Chevy with bad valves, busted shocks, and 150,000 miles on its rusted frame. Cars pack the thrill of speed, masculine power, control, and the freedom of mobility, all in one big machine where a guy can be alone with a girl or cruise for action, just for the hell of it.

Another of Chet's talents is his ability to keep everyone laughing, even in the darkest circumstances, even if the laughs are at his expense. He's the constant brunt of most jokes, made because he eats so, so much. He's called "fat," "a corpulent specimen," "stout," "pudgy," "fatso." In one shopping stop midway through *The Short-Wave Mystery,* the growing boy buys a handful of chocolate bars, a bottle of lemon soda, half a pound of fig crackers, three oranges, two ice cream cones, and a small bottle of pickles, all of which he wolfs down.

But Chet's odd projects and love of food often help solve mysteries. So, even though he complains about being tired and does everything in his power to pass his work on to others, Chet Morton is always ready to join the chase in his noisy yellow jalopy. He may heave a loud sigh of relief when the adventures come to a temporary end, but he sure misses Frank and Joe when they're not around.

The gang's he-man is Biff Hooper, who keeps his "muscles like steel" in shape by boxing and swinging at punching bags and shadows. Everything's big about this lanky, blond six-footer—even his dog, a Great Dane named Tivoli. Biff's a lifeguard and a member of the wrestling team; he owns a boat called the *Envoy* and has a blue coupe and a secondhand jeep. No wonder all the girls flirt with him, as in *The Phantom Freighter:*

> *"Oooh! Such muscles!" said the young lady admiringly. . . . Turning to Biff she remarked again, "Such muscles!" Joe grinned. . . . Crimson with embarrassment, Biff fled. Out in the street he glared at Joe Hardy. "If you tell any of the fellows at school. . . . Can I help it if I have biceps? . . . Don't tell anyone what that dizzy girl said."*

No girls lust after Phil Cohen, the "diminutive, black-haired Jewish boy," the only gang member headed for college. He's given to ethnic utterances like "Oy, what a fine day you pick for your trip!" as he does in *The Missing Chums*. Quiet and intelligent, Phil is so sensitive that he paints and draws. But this artistic braniac wouldn't be part of the Hardy gang unless he were willing to swing his fists and hold his own. In a scuffle he's agile, fearless, even reckless, just like another ethnic pal—the dark-haired, olive-skinned Tony Prito, the son of Bayport's prosperous Italian building contractor. Born in Italy, Tony has some trouble speaking Bayport English early on, because, as we read in *The Tower Treasure*,

> *[H]e had not yet been in America long enough to talk the language without an accent, and his attempts were frequently the cause of much amusement to his companions. He was quick and good-natured, however, and laughed as much at his own errors as any one else did.*

"What's the mattah?" he asks Frank and Joe when they ask for his help in distracting the chief of police. As a chum, he's useful: his continental heritage comes in mighty handy when it's time for someone to play the accordion, and when Tony tries to pass himself off as a native of Guatemala in *The Clue in the Embers* (1955), he looks the part. He's an amiable and dexterous guy, a whiz on the parallel bars and when it comes to fixing anything mechanical. At the wheel of the boat that he's proudly named the *Napoli,* he's a helmsman with nerves of iron. In times of crisis, Tony Prito is someone to count on, a boy as good as his word.

The Hardys' boy friends are important throughout the series, but because the preteen kids reading the Hardy Boys are not particularly interested in romance, the presence of girls in the mysteries is insignificant. They have to make an appearance, of course, for otherwise the Hardy Boys and their pals' sexuality would be a little suspect. Frequent cameos are made by Iola Morton, Chet's sister, who is as cute and slender as her brother is fat. She plays the violin, has a puppet named Little Red Riding Hood, and can converse about the finer points of baseball. She's sweet on Joe, but while he admits that "she's the most interesting girl in town," he's still not ready to kiss her.

Frank is the brother more apt to cast an appreciative eye on the other sex, and when he does, it falls on brown-eyed, brown-haired, vivacious Callie Shaw. She's a looker, with small, even, dazzling white teeth, a girl who brings jars of homemade jellies to lonely widows and is so smart that she's named high school valedictorian. She's "an object of special enthusiasm with Frank," but she doesn't get kissed either.

Young teen girls like the thrill of romance, not the ickiness of sex, and that may explain why Nancy Drew's a little bit blasé on the subject of romance. When she first sees a tall, handsome guy moving her car in *The Clue in the Diary,* she suspects him of stealing it and calms down only when she figures out that Ned Nickerson is just

trying to be helpful. And being helpful, in fact and alas, blossoms into a full-time job for the guy. Ned's no boy; he's a college man, and a dreamboat at that, with his dark, slightly curly hair, tender eyes, and college sweater and football jersey. When he looks at Nancy, her heart thumps loudly. It's love at first sight, from his perspective and hers, at least for a while. After the fuss about the car, Nancy moons over this all-American boy with the take-charge manner:

> *After Ned had hung up the receiver, Nancy fairly danced back into the bedroom. She sent one slipper flying toward the bed, and the other into the far corner of the room. She attempted to explain her jubilant spirits by telling herself that she was overjoyed at unearthing a possible clue to the identity of the person who had caused the Raybolt fire.*

Ned's just a one-book crush, though, because as hunky and helpful as he is, Nancy's ardor cools and she soon takes Ned for granted. She and Ned may share candlelit dinners, go on moonlight strolls, take boat trips and hayrides, and attend tea dances in book after book, but from Nancy's perspective, they're never more than "special friends."

Nancy's indifference doesn't faze Ned: he even organizes a gala barbecue in Nancy's honor before she heads down to South America in *The Mystery of the Brass-Bound Trunk* (1940), a trip on which she takes her cat but not him. And she doesn't wonder if he's being a wimp or is just a liberated guy when he says, "Anything you do is all right with me."

And Ned does all right. Carson Drew believes him to be a fine young fellow; his teammates hoist him atop their shoulders after he scores a crucial touchdown, and his Omega Chi Epsilon fraternity brothers elect him their president. Nancy's just not as excited about him as the guys are, and she's not interested to share in his spotlight. Nancy doesn't need Ned. She's got her own car and money and is too busy to be needy. To be honest, Nancy knows

that Ned's got nowhere else to go; he lives to serve her and isn't interesting enough to merit a book series of his own.

Interestingly, food's the great leveler in Nancy's world, integral to deepening friendships and fueling a hard day's work. Hearty breakfasts—orange juice, soft-boiled eggs, buckwheat cakes, and buttered toast—help Nancy and the girls keep up their energy. Luncheons of cold cuts, potato salad, chicken salad with ripe tomatoes, toasted cheese sandwiches with *lots* of paprika, tasty salads with cucumbers often provide the only times that the girlfriends get a chance to catch their breath. Teatime is a moment for cool drinks and dainty sandwiches, a cup of bouillon with a *speck* of nutmeg, the time to sum up afternoon events and pause for reflection. When work is done and dinner's served, it's likely to be substantial—duck stuffed with apples, broiled chicken, or roast lamb with mashed potatoes and fresh peas. As founding members of the Clean Your Plate Club, Nancy and her friends never skip dessert—scrumptious ice cream, chocolate mousse, pumpkin pie, raspberry tarts, puddings, or zesty orange ices.

The Hardy Boys and their friends eat a lot more and a lot more often than Nancy Drew and her pals: the series features hearty lunches packed by Mrs. Hardy, snacks eaten on the run, and provisions picked up at general stores, as well as full-fledged, sumptuous, sit-down dinners and late-night suppers served up by housekeepers and grateful clients. The boys lust for meat—roast beef, venison, hamburgers, pork, and chicken—and although they live near the water, they barely touch fish. They stuff themselves on heavy comfort food—soups, ham and eggs, sausages, potatoes that are fried or creamy and mashed, succotash, man-sized sandwiches, flapjacks, and cornbread. Each repast is topped off with mounds of desserts, including fresh-baked cakes, rich lemon pies frothy with meringue, pyramids of cookies and doughnuts, and Bigloo Igloo ice-cream sundaes crowned with nuts, whipped cream, and cherries, all washed down with fragrant coffee, rich, steaming cocoa, or fruit punch. They sniff out food everywhere: when they work on a case in Puerto Rico in *The Ghost at Skeleton Rock,* they eat lip-smacking arroz con pollo at El Calypso Caliente; while driving through Maryland in *The Secret of the Lost Tunnel* (1950), they pull off the road for Dinah's Fried Chicken. When an Automat opens in downtown Bayport in *What*

Happened at Midnight, city and country boys alike marvel as they drop nickels into slots and lift up the thick glass doors to get their slices of apple pie.

Wherever adventures take Nancy Drew and the Hardy Boys, wherever the sleuths come and go with friends, they, like most teens, always return at the end of the day to the safety and comfort of home. At the Hardy home, mother Laura is rarely around—she doesn't like to stay home alone and often goes off to visit family members. When she does stay in, this nervous, pale, tight-lipped woman sits anxiously by the telephone, waiting for it to ring. She sits up all night in bed, alone and awake, worrying, worrying, worrying about her boys and husband.

A sense of life and maternal concern is vested in the person of Aunt Gertrude, Fenton's spinster sister. Her appearance in *The Missing Chums* sets up her character:

> *Aunt Gertrude was one of the pepperiest and most dictatorial old women who ever visited a quiet house-*

hold. *She was a rawboned female of sixty-five, tall and commanding, with a determined jaw, an acid tongue, and an eye that could quell a traffic cop. She was as authoritative as a prison guard, bossed everything and everybody within reach, and had a lofty contempt for men in general and boys in particular.*

A first-class pessimist, Gertrude Hardy visits frequently at the beginning of the series, before she invites herself to move in and take over the guest bedroom. Crotchety Gertrude crochets, reads Longfellow, and runs the Bayport Historical Society. She also bellows, bawls people out, and gives Frank and Joe hell when they don't do what she thinks they should. But the fact is that Aunt Gertrude loves the boys dearly, and Frank and Joe get the message—not through icky kisses, but by Gertrude's constant fussing and her willingness to serve up the best food in town at the drop of a hat. Even if "don't" is her favorite word and she sometimes treats everyone in sight as if they're half-wits, Gertrude starts out as the series's tart and bony tyrant and ends up as everyone's favorite character.

At the Drew house, too, an older woman moves in to keep the home fires burning. Before her workload heated up, that had been Nancy's duty, as *The Mystery at Lilac Inn* explains:

> *Since the death of her mother many years before, Nancy had managed the household. On the whole, she had engineered everything so skillfully that her father little dreamed of the heavy responsibility which rested upon her shoulders.*

Hannah Gruen is a reliable local who speaks in the flat tones of the Midwest. She comes to the Drews when her former employers, the Tomlin Smiths, can no longer afford her services. Mrs. Gruen starts as a temp, an old, lower-class servant who cooks, cleans, and seldom speaks. In early books, no one confides in her, least of all "Miss Nancy," who's a touch brisk with the help. But as the series rolls on (and her age and weight

DON'T *call* ME *girl*

Fifty years after winning the right to vote, women in the 1970s still found themselves having to fight for equal rights. In demonstrations, they carried placards that expressed their anger, determination, and sometimes, humor, with slogans such as "Don't Cook Dinner Tonight, Starve a Rat Today."

Some feminists praise Nancy Drew as the first independent female role model in fiction for girls. But was she? One observer describing the "new woman" back in the 1920s wrote:

> *She takes a man's point of view . . . She'll drive you from the station . . . in her own little sportscar . . . she'll dive as well as you, perhaps better . . . and she'll take everything you say the way you mean it.*

Sounds a lot like Nancy Drew. With poise and agility, this liberated female had a life that was a far cry from what her mother experienced.

During the progressive era (roughly 1895–1920), many middle- and upper-class women moved into the political arena by performing "good works" for the poor. They thought of themselves as moral guardians and were dedicated to social "improvement," which included reforming the laws that kept them from voting, owning property, and obtaining birth control.

By 1910, the word *feminism* had been coined, but the movement was already well established, especially with regard to the vote—the suffrage movement had begun in the late nineteenth century. Having transformed their roles from helpmates to movers and shakers, more and more women found their nonvoting status intolerable, and protests increased by the early 1900s. With the determined picketing of Alice Paul, Carrie Chapman Catt, Elizabeth Cady Stanton, and the demands for birth control from Margaret Sanger, the

movement gained momentum. But nothing pushed women forward faster than World War I.

With 16 percent of the male workforce "over there," women filled many abandoned factory positions. Soon, 20 percent of electrical machinery, airplanes, and food were produced by women. Still more took jobs in medical facilities, and so many worked with voluntary relief organizations that women's patriotism and participation for the betterment of the country and the war effort was finally recognized: in 1921, the Nineteenth Amendment was passed, giving women the right to vote, just as the glories of consumerism were changing lives in other ways.

Ready-to-wear clothes, canned foods, and household appliances drastically altered the life of the 1920s housewife. Although in reality these so-called time-saving products often created more chores and took up more—not less—of her day, the housewife of the twenties learned from advertisements that things were easier for her than ever before. Electricity extended her working hours, meaning that she could accomplish more tasks more efficiently, and with so many luxuries creeping into the market, little rewards for a hard day's work could be bought without much struggle. The media created a new image of a never-flustered, productive, fashionable housewife.

Almost eleven million women held paying jobs by the end of the decade, and the thrill of spending their own money was not lost on them. Fashion was back. Swimsuits and slacks brought women the freedom to be active. Flappers, with their taste for luxury and iconoclasm, found models in movie stars—tough vamp Theda Bara, Clara Bow, the original "it" girl, and strong-willed young Joan Crawford, who defined "sexy" for the era. The efficient, adorned housewife, the independent working woman, and the daring flapper all helped break the old mold for women.

KIDDIE *lit* GROWS UP

In 1975, the ten favorite novels of high school students were books written for adults: *The Catcher in the Rye; Go Ask Alice; The Outsiders; To Kill a Mockingbird; A Separate Peace; Jonathan Livingston Seagull; The Lord of the Flies; Of Mice and Men; Lisa, Bright and Dark;* and *The Exorcist.*

When twenty-one-year-old Maureen Daly published her first book, *Seventeenth Summer,* in 1942, she had no idea that her tale of first love, which portrayed teenagers smoking, breaking rules, and hanging out, would become a best-seller that's still in print with over 1.5 million copies sold. The first-person narrative gave teens the sense that they were reading about their own lives, and with this book young adult literature was born.

In 1930, when kids weren't buying books for themselves and adults were deciding what they should read, the American Library Association (ALA) started compiling lists of recommended books for young adults. The books listed were either written for grown-ups or children; none were written specifically for teenagers. In 1948, largely due to the runaway success of Daly's book, the ALA had to admit that children's books had no place on its now-renamed list, "Adult Books for Young People." It wasn't until 1958 that the group formally recognized the category of "young adult" fiction. But while young adults were defined as individuals twelve to eighteen years old, defining a young adult, or YA, novel has proven complicated, because the audience for them is in constant flux, and the books themselves have to reflect a range of physical and mental capacities.

To everyone's surprise, adult novels that became classics, including Harper Lee's *To Kill a Mockingbird* (1960) and John Knowles's *A Separate Peace* (1959), did so because they were selling in large numbers to adolescents. The most well-known of these, J. D.

Salinger's masterpiece of teenage angst, *The Catcher in the Rye,* sent shock waves through the literary world in 1951 as it climbed to the top of best-seller lists. Salinger depicted a world of isolation as seen through the eyes of sixteen-year-old Holden Caulfield, a troubled youth who'd been expelled from his prep school and placed in a sanatorium. Caulfield obsesses over the hypocrisy, self-indulgence, and stupidity of society. He wants no part of the adult world of "phonies," but when he begs "don't let me disappear," he's expressing every teenager's worst fear—anonymity. Teens identified with his turmoil and still do; the book has become a teenage bible.

The Catcher in the Rye galvanized critics, adults, and teenagers. Some saw truth in its pages; others saw danger in its critical putdown of American life. Citing the passages about suicide and killing, some critics deemed the book wholly inappropriate for teens, and banned it and pulled it off library shelves. It remains controversial to this day.

If parents and librarians thought that they could mold teen temperament by banning a voice that teens identified with, they were proven wrong. By the 1960s, young adult literature was blazing into new territory with books like S. E. Hinton's *The Outsiders* (1967) and Paul Zindel's *The Pigman* (1968). The fictional teen heroes of these stories were social misfits bound together by their lack of a place in society. Young adult novels were tackling difficult subjects. Sandra Scopettone dealt with homosexuality in *Trying Hard to Hear You* (1974), Richard Peck wrote about rape in *Are You in the House Alone?* (1977). Many books spoke frankly to teens about their problems, while the stories of pregnancy, depression, drugs, abortion, divorce, and death also fed the teenage appetite for melodrama and tragedy.

The 1980s, however, saw a turnaround in young adult literature. With books such as those in the Sweet Valley High series—*Perfect Summer* (1985), one book from the series, was the first young adult book to reach the *New York Times*'s paperback best-seller list—saccharine teen heroes, whose priorities were dates and clothes, fell back in line with a conservative society.

But the most significant change that the eighties brought to young adult literature was the marketing of books directly to teenagers. Inexpensive paperback editions—available not only in bookstores, but in discount megastores, malls, supermarkets, and drugstores—were as easy to buy on impulse as snack food.

fluctuate), Hannah becomes an indispensable member of the family who gets sucked into the occasional adventure, like when she rescues Nancy from the growling jaws of a Belgian sheepdog in *The Mysterious Mannequin* (1970). She's the only maternal influence Nancy will ever know, the kindly, protective woman who sews, irons, mans phones when there's a crisis, and keeps porch lights aglow in times of darkness. She's also acknowledged as the best cook in River Heights.

Precisely because she's not Nancy's mother, Hannah's the best mother Nancy could have and the teen's closest confidante. Adolescence is the time when offspring pull away from parental authority, and so in stories for adolescents, mothers' roles are typically minimized. If Nancy's mother were alive, Nancy would probably be roped in by a mom more fearful of the world than independent Nancy is.

Hannah, from an older generation of women, is fascinated by Nancy Drew's guts. She'll never try to smother Nancy's spirit, and she can't tell her what to do because, quite simply, the girl's her boss. So, if Nancy suddenly announces that she's heading overseas, Hannah doesn't bother to ask questions; she neatly packs Nancy's steamer trunk with every outfit she could possibly need. Hannah looks on benignly as the young detective stretches or breaks the rules, and implicitly trusts Nancy to use her keen judgment to do the right thing. The only thing that throws Hannah is when her routine is upset—by Togo, Nancy's dog (who first appears in *The Whispering Statue* [1937] as a bull terrier, then in later books as a fox terrier), or the numerous pesky kittens, chickens, lobsters, and wild birds that cross her path.

Like Gertrude Hardy, Hannah Gruen is fiercely loyal to her adopted family. Don't say anything bad about Nancy or her dad around Hannah. The last time someone did, in *The Clue of the Tapping Heels* (1939), she threatened them with one of Carson's golf clubs.

From the earliest days of the Syndicate, Edward Stratemeyer wanted his literature for kids to educate as well as entertain them. Fascinating bits of esoteric information were woven through the mysteries. In the Hardy Boys stories, Chet Morton's hobbies often provide a pretext. In *The Short-Wave Mystery*, Chet lectures the boys on the finer points of mounting a stuffed otter:

> *"Nobody has ever mounted an otter correctly. Everybody mounts them as if they walked straight, and they really walk with a hunched back. So bring me one, will you, and I'll fix it right."*

NANCY DREW MYSTERY STORIES

The Bungalow Mystery

CAROLYN KEENE

In *The Phantom of Pine Hill* (1965), it's Ned Nickerson who gets to show off his college smarts when he tells Nancy that

> *"Way back in 1807 the inhabitants of the Ohio Valley found it difficult to get cash. Silver dollars were scarce and the practice grew of dividing them into eight equal wedge-shaped pieces. These fractions got the nickname of bits and from this came the phrase 'two bits,' meaning one-quarter or two-eighths of a dollar!"*

These bits of arcane knowledge about odd and interesting subjects—like rose gardening, Renaissance history, the difference between alligators and crocodiles, the latest advances in electronic technology—alert young readers that it is a good thing to be curious and that there is more to life than banal everyday experiences.

But what the Nancy Drew and Hardy Boys mysteries do best, without fanfare, hysterics, or heavy-handed moralizing, is to reinforce the values adults believe they should pass along to their kids. Bayport and River Heights are run like the city-states of ancient Greece, where youths were trained

to be strong and to cheerfully assume responsibility in their communities. The worlds created by Franklin W. Dixon and Carolyn Keene are really no different, and Nancy and the Hardy Boys don't have to suffer through civics classes or sit still for lectures on responsibility from their parents. What they learn, they don't learn in school. They learn through their adventures, on the street, and in the School of Hard Knocks. High school, the hub of most teens' lives where they hang out and hide out, is pushed to the farthest edge of Nancy's universe and barely intrudes on Frank and Joe's workload.

The code of behavior that these upstanding American teenagers live by is as old as the Ten Commandments, as sacrosanct as the Pledge of Allegiance. For Nancy Drew and the Hardy Boys, character is destiny. Their values are clear, strong, and unshakable. Nancy, Frank, and Joe don't need to be asked to take on responsibility; they're the first to volunteer. They take risks and roll with the punches, work hard, and have clear goals, and they never, ever give up. And for that they're always rewarded. They also make it clear that violence in thought, words, and action has no place in life and that it's important to be compassionate and to give people a chance.

Kids who love to read the books—to escape, enjoy a good story, use their imaginations, solve a mystery—can't help but admire the young detectives' examples of how far a boy or girl can get if they learn to trust themselves and be who they really are. Frank, Joe, and Nancy show kids what can happen if they're not afraid of the unknown, and they stand firm in their conviction that the ends *never* justify the means and that good will triumph over evil. So, there's never a reason to lie, cheat, or play dirty, because in a world where all plots lead to happy endings, where all troubles are resolved, nothing's ever as bad as it seems. That's what keeps kids coming back for more.

giving up he suddenly swung down the por
pillar and began to gather up the peanut
Closer and closer he came to Nancy until sl
was able to reach out and grab him. Jock
squirmed in her grasp, but as soon as he disco

CHAPTER 3

The Living End

By the late 1950s, the Stratemeyer Syndicate knew that it was time to overhaul the classic but middle-aged Nancy Drew and Hardy Boys books. As satellites circled the earth, suburbia seduced families away from cities, and teenagers took over American culture, Nancy, Frank, and Joe were no longer the coolest teens around. Adolescence was now experienced earlier and earlier; kids were growing up faster and faster with each passing year. Movies made for teens, like Blue Denim (1959), and magazines that ran the gamut from *Calling All Girls* to *MAD* to *True Confessions,* dazzled increasingly sophisticated kids with a cornucopia of new products, giving them the inside track on music, dating, and grooming. Teens were formidable new consumers who were scrutinized, courted, and catered to by manufacturers and the media. With $9 billion to spend on themselves, teenagers watched television commercials and listened to advertising in between the songs that played on their transistor radios, studying every ad that caught their eye or traded on their insecurities.

Every afternoon when kids rushed home after school, it wasn't to do homework or to read a book, but to practice doing the stroll in front of their console televisions, mimicking Justine and Bob on *American Bandstand,* or later in the evening, to watch transfixed as new teen stars like Ricky Nelson solved *their* neatly scripted problems in less than thirty minutes. By 1960, 85 percent of the homes in the country had television sets, which were pulling

audiences away from reading of all sorts. For teens who loved to loaf around, TV did all the work, "nourishing" them with entertainment on a regular feeding schedule. No need to turn pages and concentrate or imagine what a favorite action hero looked like; stimulating theme songs, catchy words, and bright images flew by, punctuated by even faster and more ingeniously produced commercials that had their own stories to tell about what it took to be cool, sexy, and popular.

Kids' growing addiction to television put a big dent in book sales. Nancy Drew and Hardy Boys mysteries, still Grosset & Dunlap's best-sellers, were slipping. They were not alone: the popularity of serial books had peaked in the mid- to late 1950s and would decline through the 1970s. As a result, publishers hacked away at their lists. The Connie Blair Mystery Series, starring a young advertising woman, got the ax in 1958. Once-popular Judy Bolton died off in 1967, and Cherry Ames took her last breath in 1968. Boys' series heroes died young, too: Ken Holt (1949–63), Rick Brant (1947–68), Chip Hilton (1948–66), and finally Tom Swift Jr. (1954–71). Surviving series books, steppingstones in the development of mass teen entertainment, would have to get in step with contemporary life if they were to survive.

One way for publishers to feed the story pipeline with appealing books for the massive, hip, and discerning baby-boom market was to put a fresh spin on old brand names and familiar characters. Having already steered the Stratemeyer Syndicate through two tumultuous decades of teen fads and fashions, Harriet Adams, now running the Syndicate on her own, saw the writing on the wall: the Hardy Boys and Nancy Drew needed to be updated as characters and the books needed to expand into other media if they were to keep pace with kids and a changing economy.

Back in the late 1930s, Adams had flirted with the idea of making Nancy Drew a bigger star with the help of Hollywood, when Warner Brothers paid the Syndicate $6,000 for the rights to bring the young sleuth to the silver screen. If Andy Hardy, played by a young Mickey Rooney, was everyone's favorite boy next door, let Nancy, a girl who had already proved her popularity in print, give him a run for his money. The studio cast Bonita Granville, who specialized in playing brats, to star as Nancy. The series of four screwball B-movies that emerged bore little relationship to the books, although in some ways, Nancy's world *did* come alive in the short, sixty-five-minute, black-and-white films. Moviegoers got to see her canopy bed, her speeding roadster, and Carson's rose garden. If mystery elements were downplayed, plots simplified, and the romance spiced up, if Ned Nickerson's name was changed to the more popular "Ted," if Bess and George were axed but song-and-dance numbers added to make Nancy Drew's world more entertaining, well, that's show biz.

In August 1939, Harriet Adams wrote to Mildred Wirt about Wirt's favorable response to *Nancy Drew, Detective*, a film based on *The Password to Larkspur Lane* (1933):

> *I am glad that you enjoyed the moving picture . . . . I have only seen the first two, although three have been shown in this area, and I have just heard that a fifth is in production. Up to date we have not found that having Nancy Drew on the screen has increased the sale of the books any, but perhaps it takes a while to get these things started.*

Edward Stratemeyer—a nineteenth-century visionary who made his fortune exploiting mass production to build a children's entertainment empire—probably would have cheered to see Nancy, Frank, and Joe leap from one medium to another. As early as 1917, Stratemeyer had tried to stir up interest by circulating a movie treatment for the Tom Swift series. But it was only after

As important as the texts, covers for both the Nancy Drew and Hardy Boys mysteries reflect the changing fads and fashions of the fickle teen market. The Hardys' *The Sinister Signpost* has had three covers *(opposite)*. The original of 1936 was revised in 1950 and again in 1968. The action's gotten hotter with each revision. Nancy Drew's adventure *The Secret in the Old Attic* (1944) underwent cover modernizations in 1962 and 1970. Many of the covers no longer illustrate scenes from the books, but they are a whole lot scarier.

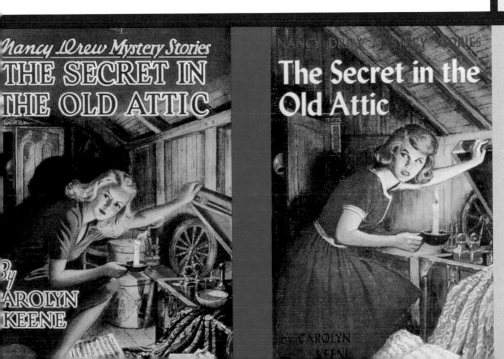

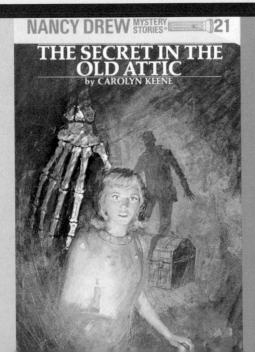

World War II that a younger visionary, Walt Disney, figured out how to take children's entertainment into uncharted ground. Disney hired artists and technicians, and through new storytelling technologies, harnessed the newest media to give renewed life to old fairy-tale personalities like Snow White and Pinocchio, characters he had enlivened in films in 1937 and 1940. Under his direction, cartoon characters like Mickey Mouse and Donald Duck, and even Cinderella, soon hopscotched from movies to television, from books to toy stores and supermarkets, and, finally, to the ultimate fantasy destination—Disneyland.

Like Stratemeyer, Disney was attracted to the values embodied in larger-than-life adventure heroes, and understood their hypnotic power over American audiences. By the 1950s, Disney and his executives decided that the company's new ABC-TV program, *Disneyland,* should feature an American hero as the subject of a live-action miniseries. They tossed around folk heroes like Johnny Appleseed and Daniel Boone, and by dumb luck, settled on frontiersman Davy Crockett's legendary rags-to-riches life—from his birth on a mountaintop in Tennessee to his election to Congress to his death defending the Alamo. Crockett's saga was a Horatio Alger–sized success. After five installments aired in 1954, its theme song, "The Ballad of Davy Crockett," topped the record charts. The TV segments were then quickly repackaged as a feature-length movie, *Davy Crockett, King of the Wild Frontier* (1955), which set off a $100 million buying frenzy as little boomer kids grabbed up Crockett "coonskin" caps and fringed jerkins.

A year later, another popular Disney TV show, *The Mickey Mouse Club,* looking for wholesome characters to feature in its live-action shorts, zeroed in on the Hardy Boys. Disney paid $5,700 to Grosset & Dunlap and the Stratemeyer Syndicate for the broadcast rights to produce nineteen

SCREEN TEENS

Andy Hardy, *opposite, top left*—no relation to Frank and Joe—was the silver screen's most famous teen in the late 1930s and 1940s. Mickey Rooney played the fumbling, good-natured character, whose adventures in such films as *Love Finds Andy Hardy* (1938) revolved around young misses played by other teens, including Judy Garland and Lana Turner.

A Clockwork Orange (1971), *above left,* chilled audiences with its depiction of a gang of violent teenagers run amok in a nightmarish but stylishly futuristic world. The kids trashed homes and maimed, humiliated, and killed adults for sheer exhilaration.

The story of a middle-aged man's sexual obsession with a teenage girl, Stanley Kubrick's *Lolita* (1962), *above middle,* translated Vladimir Nabokov's scandalous novel to film. The movie starred James Mason and Sue Lyon, who said that playing the nymphet changed her life, but not for the better.

Wealthy teen shopaholic Cher Horowitz (Alicia Silverstone) was featured in *Clueless, above right,* Hollywood's irreverent adaptation of Jane Austen's nineteenth-century novel *Emma.* This 1995 remake is set in Beverly Hills and focuses on Cher's desire to rise above her self-indulgence in a world filled with other teen girls who look like models and talk like Valley girls.

Hollywood banked on ingenue Bonita Granville, shown in *Nancy Drew, Detective, left,* to score box office gold as Nancy and give Andy Hardy a run for his money as the most popular teen on the silver screen. Director William Clemens made four Nancy Drew mystery movies, all released by Warner Brothers: *Nancy Drew, Detective; Nancy Drew, Reporter; Nancy Drew, Troubleshooter;* and *Nancy Drew and the Hidden Staircase.* Produced in 1938 and 1939, these B-movie features were critical and popular successes, but had only very tenuous connections to the plots of the books. One critic reviewing *The Hidden Staircase* said the only similarity between the book and the film was the word *staircase.*

MAKEOVER ARTISTS

Russell Tandy based the first illustrations of Nancy Drew on a New York model named Grace Horton.

It was Russell Tandy, a fashion illustrator and drinking buddy of Salvador Dali, who gave Nancy Drew her glamorous blonde hair and shapely legs. Tandy drew Butterick sewing patterns and Sears Roebuck catalogue outfits before he was hired to illustrate the first Nancy Drew covers in 1929. Over his twenty-year career, he designed twenty-six covers for the Nancy Drew series and five for the Hardy Boys.

It took more than a few illustrators to figure out the right look for the Hardy Boys. One of the first who tried was Walter S. Rogers, who played up the stories' adventure angle and made the brothers look like gnomes racing through rough landscapes. Later in the 1930s, J. Clemens Gretta and Paul Laune moved in closer and turned the spotlight on Frank and Joe, dressing the boys in big-shouldered detective suits. Gretta and Laune's more sophisticated illustrations evoked a shadow-filled art deco atmosphere of mystery. After World War II, advertising illustrator Bill Gillies punched up the covers of both series, and readers got a more casual Nancy, Frank, and Joe, who seemed a little more relaxed.

Rudolph (Rudi) Nappi took over cover designs for both series in 1953, and was the last illustrator to have a major say in the look of the teen detectives. Nappi worked on both series for so long—he completed 150 color covers over thirty years—that he wound up updating his own illustrations. A designer of sexy covers for men's magazines, Nappi buffed up Frank and Joe to look like TV stars, and made Nancy look like Sandra Dee. His last Nancy Drew cover was *The Thirteenth Pearl* and last Hardy Boys cover *The Sting of the Scorpion*, both published in 1979.

fifteen-minute segments that would tell two Hardy Boys stories. The first episode of *The Mystery of the Applegate Treasure*, based on *The Tower Treasure*, aired on October 1, 1956. *The Mystery of the Ghost Farm*, an original script, followed in 1957. *The Mickey Mouse Club* was aimed at young children and preteens, and Frank and Joe, played by Tim Considine and Tommy Kirk, looked the part. Although the stars were fifteen, they appeared to be younger than the brothers in the books and closer in age to the kids tuning in to *The Mickey Mouse Club*.

Soon, kids were buying their way into the Hardy Boys gang and Disney was spinning off merchandising articles, boosting the characters to greater visibility and success. The Syndicate was benefiting from the revitalization and increased popularity of its thirty-year-old characters as well as from the royalties generated by coloring books, comic books, flicker rings, and even a board game based on the Disney shows.

This time, for once, it was Nancy Drew who took a backseat to the Hardy Boys. Parker Brothers issued The Nancy Drew Mystery Game in 1957, but except for that and, years later, a jigsaw puzzle (1978), a doll (1978), *The Nancy Drew Cookbook: Clues to Good Cooking* (1973), *The Nancy Drew Private Eye Diary* (1979), *The Nancy Drew Sleuth Book* (1979), and various activity and coloring books, Nancy kept her upper-class nose out of the coarse world of merchandising.

The Hardy Boys were a hit on *The Mickey Mouse Club*, but any kid watching TV daily and going to the movies on Saturday afternoons in the late 1950s might have found it difficult to identify with Frank and Joe and their quaint world as it was described in the old-fashioned books written decades earlier. The same held true of Nancy. The fact that these mystery stories had remained popular for so long, with virtually no revisions,

was a tribute to how well constructed they were in the first place. But what one nostalgic generation of adults considers timeless can look dated to a new generation of kids. The late 1950s—when middle-class kids were eating TV dinners and the civil rights movement was percolating—was no time for Nancy Drew to still be sitting down to tea sandwiches or for the Hardy Boys to be fearful of "menacing Negroes" or distrustful of shady characters with foreign accents.

To hold on to kids still interested in reading, Harriet Adams and her right-hand man, Andrew Svenson, who'd joined the Syndicate a decade earlier as a writer and editor, rolled up their sleeves, and with the help of three secretaries, got to work updating the Hardy Boys and Nancy Drew mysteries, starting with the first book in each series. It was Adams's smartest move—or the worst decision she ever made, according to die-hard fans of the "classic" books—to undertake the series' major overhaul, an eighteen-year commitment.

The opportunity was unique for Adams. While the Syndicate could cut costs by shortening the books and modernizing production, by revising

and editing earlier texts and writing most of the new Nancy Drew books, Harriet Adams could finally claim authorship for herself. At the same time, the Syndicate could address complaints from the parents of some readers, who objected to the racial stereotyping that had riddled the books since their introduction. But whether driven by concern for the Syndicate's health, social conscience, or her own ego, it's clear that if Adams hadn't had the guts and the smarts to refashion the Syndicate's classic characters, there would have been no more cliff-hangers for Nancy, Frank, and Joe. They would have died a sad, slow, death and contributed three more tombstones to the graveyard of children's series literature.

In truth, the original stories weren't so much revised as they were gutted and, in some cases, totally rewritten by Adams, Svenson, and various freelance writers. Some of the original texts *were* truly dated. In 1930, when *The Great Airport Mystery* was published, few readers had flown in an airplane and therefore found it exciting that the Hardy Boys used a propeller to chase crooks. Hipper plot lines replaced antiquated ones. *The Flickering Torch* (1943), originally about a strange signal that flickered on and off from a mountaintop, was rewritten in 1971 to feature a rock group called the Flickering Torch.

The Syndicate soft-pedaled the radical surgery being performed on all Nancy Drew and Hardy Boys books written prior to the late fifties. It told girls picking up the revised 1959 edition of the 1930 classic *The Secret of the Old Clock* that "This new, modern story, based on the original title, *The Secret of the Old Clock,* has been written for the enjoyment of the girl of today," while Franklin W. Dixon claimed that the new versions of the Hardy Boys mysteries had been changed to "give his readers the most up-to-date methods of crime detection."

SUBSCRIBING *to* COOLNESS

OCTOBER 1953
35 CENTS IN US AND CAN
40 CENTS ELSEWHERE

THE
SEVENTEEN
LOOK
and ways
to have it

The immediate success of *Seventeen* magazine proved that teens had enough economic clout to buy out all 400,000 copies of the first issue in two days.

In February 1998, the school superintendent in a town on New York's Long Island yanked the magazines *Seventeen, Teen,* and *YM* from a middle school's library shelves, claiming, "We have a right and an obligation as educators to protect the children from sexual material that we deem to be age-inappropriate." It's strange and shocking to see *Seventeen,* the publication that virtually invented the teenage girl, on a roster of banned magazines. The brainchild of Helen Valentine, *Seventeen* premiered in 1944, and sold out the 400,000 copies of its first issue in two days. Just over a year later, its circulation topped one million, as Valentine almost single-handedly created a brand-new product: teen magazines.

An early promotional piece for *Seventeen* pictured a teenage girl and asked advertisers to "Meet Teena . . . no one thought she could read." Teena not only read, but she bought stuff, too. "Count on her to convince her parents she needs a new hat, a new dress, a complete spring wardrobe," the promotion went on. "Watch her go into the nation's stores with her friends."

Besides clothes, *Seventeen*'s Teena bought cosmetics, food (supermarkets like A&P were regular *Seventeen* advertisers in the 1950s), records, sewing kits and machines, jewelry, and even cars. Where did she get the money? "The movie Teena wants to see is the movie her boyfriend takes her to see." And she also had "money of her own to spend . . . and what her allowance and pin-money earnings won't buy, her parents can be counted on to supply. For our girl Teena won't take no for an answer when she sees what she wants in *Seventeen.*"

Not to be outdone, other publishers zeroed in on *Seventeen*'s market. In 1957, *16,* a magazine for girls "too old for daddy's knee, but too young for the boy next door," made its debut. Said Gloria Stavers, *16*'s first editor, "Just because a girl is interested in dumb stuff like the color of a boy's eyes . . . doesn't make her dumb." Still, Stavers filled the magazine with stories about young male singers and movie stars—their favorite clothes, movies, songs, the kind of girl they'd like to marry—and became a pioneer in teen celebrity publishing. Ever since, magazines like *Calling All Girls, Tiger Beat, Cool, Teenville, Dig, Teen Hop,* and *Sassy* have followed, each trying to strike it rich in the adolescent market.

The magazines that have survived have changed over time in order to keep up with rapidly evolving teen life. *Seventeen,* which ignored rock 'n' roll in the early years, finally recognized its existence in the late 1950s and admitted that it might be good background music for such tasks as stenography and typing, but warned against listening to it during serious study, since it could "make you throw down your pencil and dance."

And with everything in American culture moving faster, why shouldn't the mysteries that Nancy and Frank and Joe investigated? Syndicate writers had always been instructed to end chapters with cliff-hangers, a holdover from the days of serial literature, when each installment of a story ended with "To be continued. . . ." Now, with the number of chapters in each title chopped from twenty-five to twenty, and with stories that used to run more than 200 pages trimmed back 20 percent, action needed to rush forward even faster, at the expense of plot. The prolonged suspense of the early volumes, where stories started slowly and excitement built steadily, evaporated. Kids were hurled from one unrelated, action-packed mini-crisis to the next. Plots in the revised editions turned mechanical, and soon it became difficult to differentiate one story from the next. But one constant still remained: like her father before her, Adams drew the line at extreme violence and murder. Guns were always left at home; Frank and Joe were more likely to save the day by throwing a punch.

The new editions read faster, too; sentences were bare-boned, efficient, and unremittingly "peppy," to use one of Harriet Adams's favorite words. In the 1937 version of *The Clue in the Diary,* when Nancy and her friends speak, they "chortle," "flash angrily," "retort," "break off," or "mutter furiously"; the word "said" is used only six times in the first five chapters of the book. In the 1970 update, however, "said" appears thirty-two times, Nancy "shrieks" thirty-seven times, "groans" thirty times, and "calls gaily" on twenty-five different occasions. And what would post-*Sputnik* girls make of a car called a "roadster"? How could boys who watched *Dragnet* on TV dream of being pals with guys like Frank and Joe, who blurted out expressions like "jumping willigers!," "hot ziggety!," and "spin my prop!"?

TINY-SCREEN TEENS

The Mickey Mouse Club, right, premiered on October 3, 1955, with twenty-four perky, singing Mouseketeers. This hour of fun-filled TV renamed each day of the week for the fantastic events kids adored—from Circus Day to Anything Can Happen Day. The show was an enormous success with baby boomers, who could imagine themselves participating in the comedic skits, game shows, and musical numbers.

Bringing the concept of the stepfamily to prime-time TV, *The Brady Bunch* (1969–74), *middle,* was formed when lovely lady Carol and handsome fellow Mike married, uniting her three blonde daughters and his three brunette sons. Divided by gender and hair color, the school-age kids and their housekeeper, Alice, tackled hackneyed sitcom traumas for five seasons, refereed by their sunny but stern parents.

Named for the zip code of a fictional Beverly Hills high school, *Beverly Hills 90210, bottom,* brought soap opera to a drama-hungry adolescent audience beginning in 1990. Tackling issues like date rape, drug abuse, and pregnancy, *90210* pulls a world of trauma into the fantasy lives of very rich, coiffed, and privileged teens. In early episodes, twins Brenda and Brandon Walsh, transplants from Minneapolis, learn to survive in the cutthroat world of credit-card limits and fast cars.

In 1956 and 1957, the Disney TV series *The Mickey Mouse Club* ran two Hardy Boys serials, *The Mystery of the Applegate Treasure,* based on the first Hardy Boys mystery, *The Tower Treasure,* and *The Mystery of Ghost Farm,* an original teleplay. Young Disney regulars, Tommy Kirk and Tim Considine, *opposite,* played the Hardy brothers and appealed to a grade-school audience.

Stratemeyer Syndicate books were popular worldwide. Nancy Drew was first licensed for foreign editions in the 1930s; the Hardy Boys had to wait until 1950. The books have been published in nineteen countries and translated for audiences in the Scandinavian countries, Malaysia, South Africa, Israel, Japan, Brazil, and Indonesia. In some cases, Nancy gains some local color, too: her peachy complexion is freckled in Italy, while in France, Carolyn Keene is Caroline Quine and Nancy is known as Alice Roy. She's called Paula in Finland. The Hardy Boys become Miguel and Ricardo Maia in Portuguese editions.

Gone were the leisurely styled, evocative words and phrases that kids savored in the early texts, at a time when entertainment was harder to come by. The images that the original writers had conjured up in rich, layered language—of amnesiacs, clumsy farm boys, gothic mansions, primordial forests and glens—were just too slow for kids whose attention spans were growing shorter.

In the older books that the Syndicate was revising, and in new titles that it was commissioning, the books' form and content were changing because the world was changing. Most important, the characters had to be rejiggered to reflect the biggest change of all—what it meant to be a modern teen. Not surprisingly, updating the Hardy Boys' characters was a fairly easy task, because they were "normal," stereotypical male action heroes locked into a state of eternal, excitable boyhood. No matter what decade they lived in, Frank and Joe could cavort with pals, tinker with whatever neat gadgets were around, eat when they were hungry, and every once in a while, have a good fight. As a tight twosome, they were absolved of the longings, doubts, or opportunities that real-life teens had to struggle with individually. No dark, conflicted, or mysterious feelings motivate their behavior. No psychological underpinnings shaped their actions or triggered weird thoughts. No one needed them to change substantially, certainly not the boys who identified with them nor the adults who liked the fact that their development was arrested, frozen in time so that readers could hold on to the memories of freedom they too once had.

The Hardy Boys—who had started out as likable, well-behaved, ordinary kids who made mistakes and were willing to bend the rules if it meant solving a case—did change in some ways in

Harriet Adams owned a collection of 2,000 dolls, but never authorized the two rare Madame Alexander dolls of Nancy Drew—one wearing a plaid coat, the other in a short jacket, both with a wrist tag that reads "I am Nancy Drew"—that slipped onto the market in 1967. Adams thought that the twelve-inch-tall dolls looked babyish, despite nylon stockings and red purse, camera, sunglasses, and binoculars. Collectors love them.

The object of the Nancy Drew Mystery Game, *below,* issued first in 1957 and again in 1959, was to figure out where Nancy was and what case she was working on. Illustrated with gothic scenes from her books, the boxed set also included mystery cards, dice, colored markers, and car tokens.

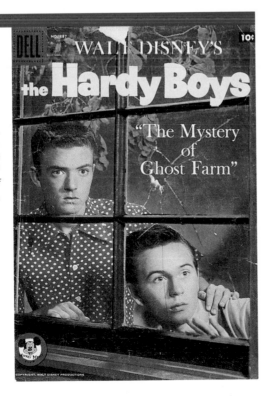

Shortly after Congress passed a comic book code in 1950, meant to keep the funnies moral and benign, Walt Disney issued four Hardy Boys comics, based on *The Mickey Mouse Club* episodes of *The Mystery of Applegate Treasure.*

the revised books: they were turned into model citizens, too good to be true. Careful to honor every law on the books, they no longer drove faster than the speed limit. By the time *The Short-Wave Mystery* was revised in 1966, Franklin W. Dixon went out of his way to make sure that the Hardy Boys and Chet had licenses to operate their shortwave radios and took their responsibilities seriously. The trappings of their lives were updated, too. Bigloo Igloo ice cream sundaes covered with nuts gave way to slices of pizza.

When it came to keeping Nancy up to date, the Syndicate had a tougher time. As originally drawn by Mildred Wirt, Nancy periodically showed herself to be a character too hot to handle, especially as America's respect for independent women waxed and waned over the decades. A stubborn tug-of-war had gone on for years between Wirt and Adams over how spunky Nancy could be. Adams won the battle when she assumed primary authorship of the series in the mid-1950s, and she began to clip Nancy's wings. The girl, who Adams had always thought was "too bold and bossy," became more decorous, more like Harriet Adams and less like Mildred Wirt. With every editorial change, every nip and tuck she made to Nancy's personality, Harriet Adams could more confidently say that *she* was the real Carolyn Keene. By 1977, all of the original Nancy Drew titles that had been written by Mildred Wirt were revised or rewritten.

In her new incarnation, Nancy was leveled out, homogenized. In the original books, readers were introduced to a nonconformist, a girl who expressed her feelings, who got angry, scared, and upset. In the revised books, Nancy is relentlessly upbeat, puts up with her father's increasingly protective tendencies, and, when asked if she goes to church in the 1969 *The Clue of the Tapping Heels,* replies, "As often as I can. . . . This morning

Dad and Hannah and I will go to service together." Nancy learns to hold her tongue; she doesn't sass the dumb cops like she used to.

As Nancy's emotions were toned down, her age shot up from sixteen to eighteen in the 1959 revision of *The Secret of the Old Clock*, to make it clear to impressionable readers that she, too, like Frank and Joe, was a law-abiding driver in every state. Then, when curvaceous Barbie dolls and overheated romance comic books began vying for little girls' attention, the Syndicate let Nancy's romantic life warm up. Slowly but surely, Nancy went from being an inspiring mythical character to a rather ordinary teenage girl.

If Adams consciously gave Nancy a new persona she was more comfortable with, she was probably less aware of how those changes were reflecting the politics of the time. In the paranoid years following Senator Joe McCarthy's anti-communist witch hunts of the early fifties, many middle-class Americans were learning to mind their manners, keep their mouths shut, respect authority, and obey the rules. In the 1950s, Nancy, too, learned to toe the line. Her larger-than-life mystique began to evaporate just as American women, who'd worked at men's jobs in factories during World War II, were being forced back into their homes, sealed off from the complex realities of cold-war life, confined to ponder the mysteries of homemaking and the joys of being good wives and perfect mothers.

Adams guarded her new creation vigilantly. Woe to any Grosset & Dunlap executive, editor, or illustrator who crossed Harriet's path or tried to dilute her new vision of Nancy Drew. Relentless, scathing letters flew from her typewriter. Adams, now seventy-one years old, cruelly chastised editors, as in this 1973 letter:

It pains me to write this letter, but you must have known I would not take your vitriolic editing of

THE GLOWING EYE without comments. I insist upon a change of attitude on your part, and would prefer not taking up this matter with your company's officers. But . . . your propensity for "red-ribbon" corrections is exceeded only by the frequency of their caustic nature. . . . Are your remarks intended to mend story holes or do you get some sadistic fun out of downgrading and offending me? . . . At a conservative estimate there are between five and six hundred adverse comments in a 170-page manuscript. . . . It will take me a long time to live down the remark "Nancy sounds like a nasty female."

The Syndicate worked hard to bring the characters up to speed by also updating the way they looked. Image-savvy teens who scoured the pages of magazines and Sears catalogs, saw fashions on television and the movies, couldn't identify with Hardy Boys in knickers. Suits and ties? Tweed caps? No way! Nancy Drew looking like Mae West? Jean Harlow? Betty Grable? Like Mickey Mouse and Betty Crocker before them, Nancy Drew and the Hardy Boys would be reconceived and redrawn. Nancy was made to look younger in the illustrations, probably because the mysteries were being read mostly by eight- to twelve-year-olds. On the beauty front, it started to look like blondes didn't always have more fun, as the color of Nancy's tresses darkened and lightened on a spectrum that ran from flaxen to titian.

Under their dust jackets, the original Hardy Boys books, bound first in red and then in brown fabric that looked like a man's suit, had a silhouette of the Hardy Boys and a lightning bolt. Old

w it's Pepsi-for those who think young

rc you find fun, you find Pepsi right at home! Its sparkling taste is so inviting, so clean. Ice-cold Pepsi-Cola drenches t, refreshes like no other. So think young ... say "Pepsi, please!"

PEPSI-COLA

In the 1920s, the few ads for teens in *Scholastic* magazine featured class rings, life insurance, and sneakers. Ten years later, the ads had gotten bigger, more frequent, and tried to sell more things, including products promising to deliver popularity. By the 1940s, Pepsi-Cola was talking to kids in their own lingo, asking "Do You Dig It?" and thereby acknowledging them as a special market. Twenty-one years later, in 1961, Pepsi made a major shift, proclaiming the beverage "for those who think young" and pitching youth as a status symbol to teenagers *and* adults alike.

Nancy Drew books were bound in her signature blue, with a logo showing Nancy sleuthing, magnifying glass in hand. A 1962 cost-cutting move disposed of the dust jackets and introduced cheaper bindings with illustrations printed directly on the front covers. Intentional or not, this move made the hardcover series look more like popular paperbacks.

Another reason for the Syndicate's extensive revision of its two most popular series was triggered by the growing concern of parents and educators who were offended by the heavy-handed treatment of minorities, the way that non-

white, non-middle-class characters were regarded with varying levels of disdain. An episode in *The Clue of the Tapping Heels* (1939) illustrates what people were complaining about:

> "Oh, you startled me!" Nancy laughed, whirling around. "I half expected to see a colored man leering at me."
>
> "Well, that's complimentary, I must say," the youth [Ned] returned with a grin. "I'm pretty sunburned but I didn't know I looked as dark as all that."

In 1924, three years before the first Hardy Boys book was released, Ku Klux Klan membership had swelled to four million Americans. When the Nancy Drew series first reached girl readers, Americans were listening to radio's most popular nightly show, *Amos 'n Andy* (1929–54). A comedy about the friendships and foibles of black men played by white actors, the program drew many of its laughs from bigoted jokes that depended on its audience believing that blacks were inferior to whites. Throughout the first third of the century, other ethnic and immigrant groups—Jews from Eastern Europe, Poles, and Italians—didn't fare much better in popular culture. Children's books of the period routinely reinforced popular myths about racial and ethnic inferiority and even about criminality.

Until the earliest books were revised, the Hardy Boys and particularly Nancy Drew were leery of people who were not like them. Black characters, like the alcoholic caretaker Jeff Tucker in *The Secret of the Old Clock* (1930), were kept in their place:

> "And a fine mess you've made of it, too. What do you think Mrs. Topham will say when she learns?"
>
> Jeff rolled his eyes.
>
> "Lawdy, Miss! What will she say? I reckon I's done gone and discharged myself."
>
> "It would be only what you deserve, Jeff. You were unfaithful to your trust."
>
> "Way you mean, Miss, trust? I don't trust nobody no mo'—especially no foot-loose white boys a-travellin'

around in see-dans. . . . Ole Jeff done gone and made a fool of himself. I realize dat whatever I gets, I's got it a-comin'."

A tear rolled out on Jeff's black, furrowed old cheek. . . .

In both series, blacks were sometimes cast as villains, sometimes as helpful secondary characters, such as the bank custodian in *Nancy's Mysterious Letter* (1932), who says, "'Scuze me, sah, but de bank am closin'. . . . Ah jest natcherly got to shet de do'."

Immigrants get similarly disparaging treatment: in the original *Nancy's Mysterious Letter,* when Nancy knocks on a neighbor's door in search of a missing mailman's pouch, it is

> [O]pened by . . . a brawny woman redolent of yellow soap and with bubbles from the washtub's suds fresh on her arms. . . .
> "Is anyone at home?" Nancy demanded. . . .
> "Not speak English, me," she smiled. "You speak maybe Polish?"
> "No, no, no!" Nancy cried. "Please try to understand. Mailman—letters—somebody steal them."

The Hardy Boys, middle-class kids, were comfortable having a few assimilated Jewish and Italian pals in their gang. And for Nancy Drew to treat anyone but a Wasp graciously, they had to know their place. Bayport and River Heights each supported bustling Chinatowns and police departments staffed by bumbling Irish cops who could barely keep the peace. Still the towns were threatened when different foreigners—swarthy-skinned exotics like Greeks, Italians, Egyptians, Japanese, Indians, and Native Americans—showed up, people with "piercing black eyes," bushy eyebrows, and facial hair. They wore dirty, flashy, or ill-fitting clothes,

and spoke too loudly and with peculiar accents guaranteed to make townspeople suspicious. When the books were revised, Harriet Adams's ethnic housekeeping was praised as a positive step, but it actually resulted in far fewer black characters in the stories, and Asian and Latin characters were more likely to work in restaurants or be witnesses to crimes rather than have the higher visibility of perpetrators.

Updates didn't stop with plots, clothes, or ethnic stereotypes. In 1959, current events set the stage for several mysteries. Hawaii was in the headlines, and Nancy Drew's thirty-sixth adventure carried this dedication:

Carolyn Keene, who knows and loves the Hawaiian Islands and laid The Secret of the Golden Pavilion *in this enchanting land, takes this opportunity of sending special greetings to the boys and girls of our fiftieth and newest state.*

That same year, Franklin W. Dixon, as patriotic as Keene, transported the Hardy Boys to Alaska for *The Mystery at Devil's Paw.*

In the earliest Hardy Boys books, the brothers stayed close to home, dealing with local crime in Bayport and its vicinity. But by the 1960s, Frank and Joe were jetting off for Mexico (*The Mystery of the Aztec Warrior* [1964]), South America (*The Masked Monkey* [1972]), Europe (*The Shattered Helmet* [1973]), Asia (*The Mysterious Caravan* [1975]), and Australia (*The Firebird Rocket* [1977]). Nancy took to the skies, too, to Scotland to meet her great-grandmother Lady Douglas in *The Clue of the Whistling Bagpipes* (1964), and to India to rescue

---

POST RULES OF NANCY DREW CLUB

The following are the rules under which the Hollywood "Nancy Drew Club" was formed, and may be the basis for yours:

1. Must have steady boy friend, in the sense of a "pal."
2. Take part in choosing own clothes.
3. No smoking, drinking, or petting.
4. Pay their share on dates with boys own age.
5. Take part in plans for own career.
6. Must have at least one hobby.
7. Must participate in at least one extra-curricular school activity.
8. Must be a high school student.

Warner Brothers created a fan club (complete with rules, *above*) to promote the 1938–39 Nancy Drew movies.

a circus elephant in the revised *Mystery of the Brass-Bound Trunk* (1976).

Did Nancy, Frank, and Joe become jet-setters because Bayport and River Heights were getting dull? Or was the Syndicate, which began seriously licensing foreign editions as early as 1937 (a Norwegian edition of *The Whispering Statue*), hoping to build a worldwide empire of young readers? By 1968, seventeen countries were translating the teen detectives' adventures. In Finland, Nancy changed her name to Paula, in Sweden she was Kitty, and in France, Alice Roy—because Nancy is the name of one of France's larger and least lovely industrial cities. But licensing was licensing, and dollars followed.

Amid all the changes being made to the books, the Hardy Boys lost most of their gang. The only one to survive as a regular character was Chet Morton, who paid a price: over time he lost his dignity, transformed into a lazy blob of a guy, the constant butt of food jokes. As the books were revised and streamlined, much of the slapstick and good-natured humor in them disappeared, too. Crusty Aunt Gertrude, with her singular brand of tough love and salty sense of humor, had the life slowly squeezed out of her.

Even the criminals were updated. Weird villains lost their quirks; Vilnoff, the deranged inventor in the 1936 version of *The Sinister Signpost* who compulsively sculpts miniature clay models of his own hands, becomes in the 1968 revision Vilno Sigor, a guy who steals designs for race cars. In the original account of *The Mark on the Door* (1934), the Hardys come face-to-face with a young girl, a victim of vicious Pedro Vincenzo, whose personal insignia is branded on her forehead. In the revised version, Vincenzo merely threatens to brand her.

But if villains become more "normal," intrigue deepens. Starting in the 1960s, the Hardy Boys

In 1969, *The Hardy Boys* cartoon *(below, top)* found animated Frank and Joe solving mysteries at a rate of two per half hour, with time in between for musical numbers with bandmates Chub Morton on the saxophone and new characters Pete Jones and Wanda Kay on the drums and tambourine.

In January 1977, Frank and Joe returned to ABC-TV in *The Hardy Boys Mysteries,* starring Parker Stevenson as Frank and Shaun Cassidy as Joe *(below, bottom).* The show ran for two years.

In March 1978, Pamela Sue Martin, disenchanted with the *Nancy Drew Mysteries* television series she was starring in, posed as Nancy Drew for *Playboy* magazine. In the softcore pictorial, millions of men got to see something Ned Nickerson never did—a very liberated Nancy in revealing nighties.

In 1977, Collegeville Costumes and Universal Studios merchandised Hardy Boys and Nancy Drew Halloween costumes based on the television versions of the characters.

become more spylike, often working with international agencies like the Pentagon and Scotland Yard. In both series, too, the IQs of the Bayport and River Heights cops increase, as Nancy and the boys put more faith in the law and in up-to-date crime-detection tools like electronic bugs and high-speed cameras.

By jettisoning their creakier aspects and reformulating the Nancy Drew and the Hardy Boys characters, the series got new leases on life and proved once again that, for the Stratemeyer Syndicate, books were business, and business came first. Purists were horrified. The books that they treasured as milestones in their reading lives had been, in their minds, defiled. But for a new generation of kids eager to read, kids who couldn't know or didn't care what they were missing, the new editions hit the right note and triggered a rush of discovery similar to what their parents had felt when they first met Nancy, Frank, and Joe decades earlier.

Overall sales for kids' series books had started to slip in the mid-1960s. Nancy Drew and the Hardy Boys were holding their own, but to understand how the market was changing, the Syndicate sponsored a survey of retail outlets, book stores, department stores, five-and-dimes, hobby shops, and discounters. From that survey, it learned that the series books were considered too expensive at $1.25 and were competing with paperbacks and TV for the attention of children who had become too sophisticated for their stories. To make matters worse, fewer kids were reading. The Syndicate began to entertain pitches from media representatives who wanted to bring the Hardy Boys back to television for a second go-around.

In 1967, an hour-long pilot version of *The Mystery of the Chinese Junk* (1960) aired on CBS, but the first adaptation to hold true to the action of Franklin W. Dixon's plot bombed. Then, in 1969, the prodigal Hardy Boys returned to the airwaves as a Saturday morning animated cartoon series. This time, mystery was set aside in favor of groovy music; Frank and Joe were members of a rock band in a show that owed a big debt to the Beatles' animated feature, *Yellow Submarine* (1968), and to *The Monkees* (1966–68), a sitcom that brought together four unknown actors to star as members of a rock group—and ended up being taken seriously as singers by fad-loving teens. The Hardy Boys as 'toons let it all hang out for two years, long enough to trigger a second wave of merchandising: another board game, activity books, and a long-playing RCA album with a psychedelic cover, *Here Come the Hardy Boys.* Corgi produced a toy truck that transported a miniature version of the rock band around floors and tabletops, and a three-reel Viewmaster set, *The Hardy Boys' Mystery of the Caves,* came with its own sixteen-page storybook.

The revisions and the visibility the Hardy Boys were getting on television and in merchandising started to pay off. In January 1973, Grosset & Dunlap sent Harriet Adams a royalty check in the amount of $143,689.88 (roughly $543,000 in 1998 dollars) for sales in the last six months of 1972, and a letter of congratulations for the most financially successful sales period in their six decades of doing business together. Two years later, a $190,442.62 check ($594,000 in 1998 dollars) for a similar royalty period was accompanied by a letter from the president of the company:

> *As I've told you on many occasions, Harriet, breaking records with you, although it is old history, is still something I regard as one of my favorite activities.*
> *I intend to rededicate myself to record breaking checks for each succeeding period.*

And he did. In 1977, the check was for $244,737.73 (roughly $678,000 in 1998 dollars).

Frank and Joe joined the ranks of boy toys Ken and GI Joe when Kenner issued these 1978 "action figures." The Frank doll, *right,* comes complete with a backpack radio.

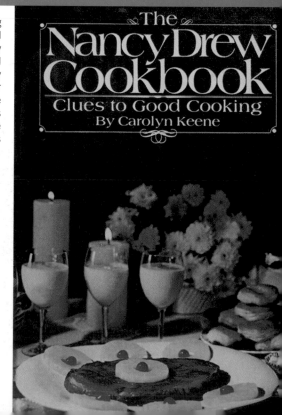

Long before eating disorders plagued teenage girls, Nancy Drew fans could cook up a tasty breakfast, lunch, or dinner following the recipes in this collection of the girl sleuth's favorite dishes.

The Nancy Drew Cookbook
Clues to Good Cooking
By Carolyn Keene

Harriet Adams could thank television for much of her series' continued success over the next few years. The live-action Hardy Boys were back on TV, and, for the first time, so was Nancy Drew. Universal Studios scored a hit in 1977 when both boys and girls tuned in to one-hour prime-time shows on ABC that alternated weekly between Nancy Drew and the Hardy Boys.

Girls shrieked for pretty-boy Shaun Cassidy, who starred as Joe Hardy, while Parker Stevenson, who played Frank, was left in the dust of the public-relations frenzy that swirled around his fictional sibling. The show featured all new stories, among them "The Strange Fate of Flight 608," in which Joe and Frank, both sporting longish, blow-dried hair, desperately attempt to pilot a plane carrying a graduating class of stewardesses through a hurricane over the Bermuda Triangle.

Meanwhile, feminists in the 1970s were on a rampage, demonstrating and lobbying for sexual, social, and political equity with men at home, at school, on the street, at work, and even on television. It was the sheer determination and organiza-tion of the movement that helped clear the path for sister Nancy to share the little screen with the Hardy Boys. Young women on TV were no longer doomed to be suffering mothers, wives, or cower-ing victims. Series like *That Girl* (1966–71), *The Mary Tyler Moore Show* (1970–77), *Police Woman* (1974–78), *Charlie's Angels* (1976–81), and *Won-der Woman* (1976–79) proved that strong women characters could score solid ratings and rake in advertising dollars. *The Nancy Drew Mysteries,* starring Pamela Sue Martin as an older, brunette Nancy working part-time on her father's payroll, premiered on February 6, 1977. At first, because the series tried to appeal to adults as well as kids, it pulled in bigger audiences than other popular crime and detective shows like *Kojak, Starsky and Hutch,* and *Barnaby Jones.*

This time around, Harriet Adams and her Syn-dicate partner Nancy Axelrad had script approval and took a more active role in the development of the series. Still, whatever liberties the producers took to make the characters more "with it" ultimately backfired with the audience. Girl fans' expectations were never quite met. Letters poured in demanding that Bess Marvin, left out of the show in the first season, get a piece of the action. Viewers didn't like George Fayne's long hair, or the fact that Ned Nickerson wasn't handsome enough, wore glasses, and was shy. In response, the show underwent fine-tuning and, then, an unheard-of format change: Nancy and the Hardy Boys were brought together to share mysteries in 1978. The ratings didn't go up, but the tempera-ture did when Pamela Sue Martin walked away from the faltering show, thumbing her nose at both Nancy Drew and propriety by posing for *Playboy* magazine.

Despite the problems plaguing their counter-part, the Hardy Boys series charged on through the summer of 1979, a success that set off a third tidal

CROSSWORD CIPHER CHICKEN

3   *cups unsweetened cracker crumbs, rolled very fine*
2   *teaspoons garlic salt*
4   *tablespoons parsley flakes*
3   *tablespoons Parmesan cheese*
2   *sticks (8 ounces) margarine*
1   *2½ pound fryer, cut into serving pieces*

Heat the oven to 375°. Place crackers between 2 pieces of wax paper. Crush with a rolling pin until very fine. Put 3 cups of crumbs into a bowl. Add garlic salt, parsley flakes, and Parmesan cheese. Mix well.

Melt margarine in a saucepan over low heat. Dip each piece of chicken into it, then roll in the crumb mixture.

Cover a cookie sheet with foil and put the chicken pieces on the sheet. Bake for 1 hour. Serves 6.

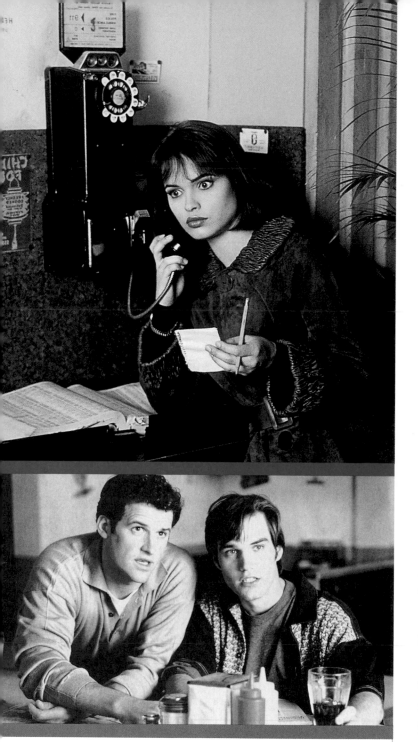

After the ABC series' demises, nearly twenty years passed before the teen sleuths were back on TV. In 1995, a Canadian production company, Nelvana, posted casting calls on the Internet and held live auditions to find the perfect new Nancy, Frank, and Joe. They found Tracy Ryan to play Nancy, Paul Popowich for Joe, and Colin Gray to be Frank. The Nancy Drew and Hardy Boys shows ran back-to-back, got lukewarm reviews, never found an audience in Canada or the States, and were canceled after one season.

wave of merchandising opportunities for another generation of boys who wanted to own a piece of the characters: yet another board game, The Secret of Thunder Mountain, was produced, as well as a second LP, *The Hardy Boys Wonderland.* Fans could choose from seven jigsaw puzzles—including the one featuring Shaun Cassidy, not as Joe, but as a baby-faced heartthrob in a Hawaiian shirt—and there were metal lunch boxes, charm bracelets, rings, wristwatches, necklaces, Frank and Joe action figures, greeting cards, guitars, Halloween costumes, denim jeans and jackets, and even bell bottoms with Shaun Cassidy's picture and auto-graph splayed across the bottom of one leg.

Frank, Joe, and Nancy's new visibility on tele-vision boosted book sales and even turned the teens into celebrities. Grosset & Dunlap and the Stratemeyer Syndicate capitalized on their notori-ety by assigning the sleuths another moneymaking assignment: to endorse the "good literature" that stodgy educators thought kids should have been reading all along. In 1978, Nancy Drew presented her "Favorite Classics"—illustrated, unabridged volumes of *Black Beauty, Heidi,* and *Grimm's Fairy Tales.* Frank and Joe were enlisted as spokesmen for more manly fare for boys: *The Adventures of Huckleberry Finn, The Adventures of Tom Sawyer,* and *Treasure Island.* But their recommendations for books were probably too dorky for the chang-ing tastes of young adult readers, who were buying paperbacks about real problems—everything from the heartaches of romance to the pitfalls of living with a single parent to the nightmares of abortion, divorce, homosexuality, and even teen suicide.

The Stratemeyer Syndicate's relationship with Grosset & Dunlap had begun in 1908, and over the decades there had been ongoing disagreements about the business end of their arrangement. Harriet Adams had been badgering, cajoling, and arguing with Grosset & Dunlap for more advertising and higher royalty rates for years. In a June 16, 1969, letter to her publishers, she argued:

> It occurred to me recently that when my father signed a contract with your company some forty years ago . . . Nancy Drew and the Hardy Boys books sold for fifty cents and he received a royalty of two cents; in other words four per cent.
>
> Since that time the rate has never changed, which makes a unique situation in publishing. Don't you agree that it is high time we update our thinking in line with present day practices and increase the percentage of royalty to world renowned Carolyn Keene [and] Franklin W. Dixon?

Even though the Syndicate was earning record income from its books, Harriet was frustrated in her negotiations with Grosset & Dunlap, which she felt were going nowhere. She'd been disappointed when the seventy-fifth anniversary of the Bobbsey Twins came and went without any publicity from the publisher, and when Adams asked what the company had planned for Nancy Drew's upcoming fiftieth anniversary, she got shrugs. So she decided to play hardball and switched camps in 1979, signing a contract for the next books in both detective series with Simon & Schuster, which agreed to publish the titles and to advertise and market them aggressively. Furious at the potential loss of one of their biggest money-making series, Grosset & Dunlap sued both the Syndicate and Simon & Schuster for $300 million, claiming that because the books weren't really written by Stratemeyer and because they, Grosset & Dunlap, had originally paid the fees for the illustrations in the books, they shared in the copyright and ownership of the characters. Actually, they hadn't paid for drawings, at least in the early decades of the series.

The case went to trial, and in an exciting moment of courtroom drama, Mildred Wirt Benson, who had written the original Nancy Drew stories, came to New York to testify and set history and the legal record straight by claiming primary authorship for them; for years, Harriet Adams had been taking public credit for being Carolyn Keene. When Benson appeared in the courtroom, the patrician Adams's only comment to her was, "I thought you were dead."

When the dust settled, Grosset & Dunlap was allowed to continue publishing revised versions of the first fifty-eight Hardy Boys and first fifty-six Nancy Drew mysteries, which they reprint to this day. The Syndicate, which won the right to select the publisher of its choice to produce new stories in paperback or hardcover, proceeded to work with Simon & Schuster to publish new titles in both series. And publish they did. The first Simon & Schuster book, Nancy Drew's *The Triple Hoax*, hit stores in late 1979. Next came the Hardy Boys' *Night of the Werewolf*, and very quickly, the young detectives' caseloads were upped to four to six books in each series being published every year, a dramatic departure from the Syndicate's one-book-per-year-per-series tradition dating back to the 1930s.

Two years of legal troubles took a toll on eighty-seven-year-old Harriet Adams, but she did rally for the festivities celebrating Nancy Drew's fiftieth birthday in 1980, and some of Nancy's star power rubbed off on her. Major newspapers, national magazines, and public radio programs covered events in which Adams was proclaimed a national treasure, and Nancy was honored for her profound influence on the lives of American women.

Adams died in 1982, and the former loyal employees she had made partners in 1974 continued running the Syndicate until they finally sold the business outright to Simon & Schuster in 1984 in a mid-seven-figure deal. It was the right time to sell: In the mid-1980s, the publishing

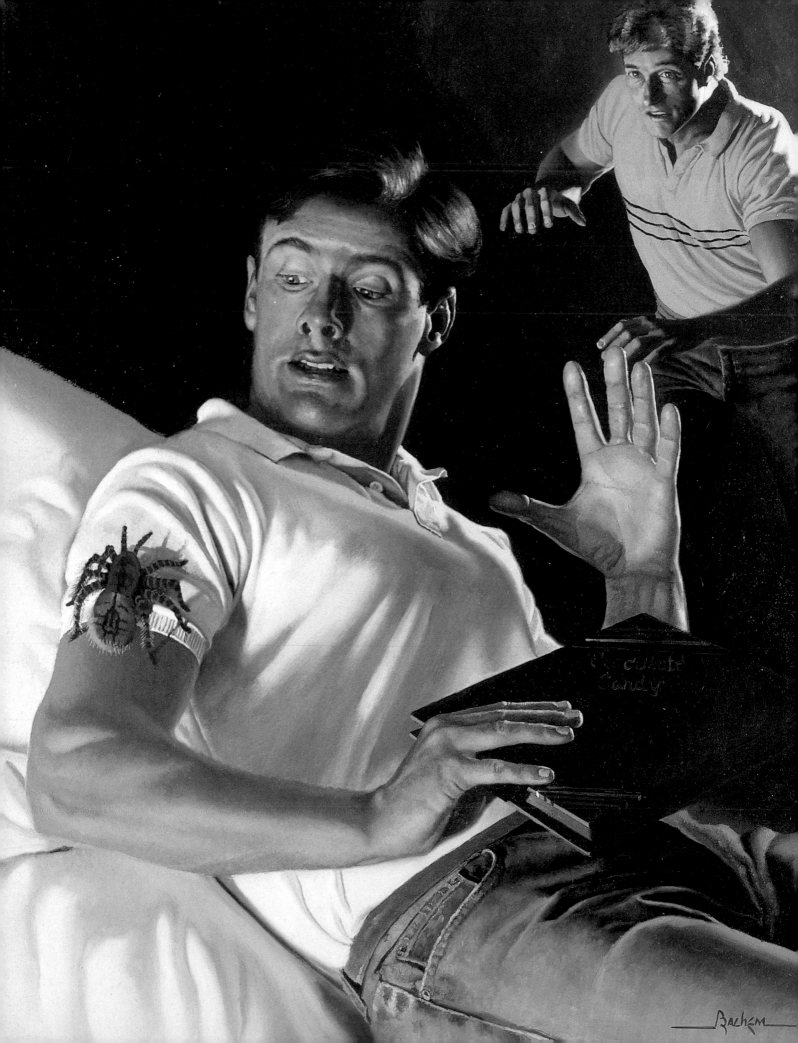

industry was in turmoil, and with an information revolution brewing, kids were discovering many more compelling ways to fill their leisure time. Kids were glued to the 155 million television sets in America. Video arcades, where they could play Pac-Man and Centipede, were more crowded than libraries. Still, new book series were launched, and those that went on to become unprecedented mass-market successes were more lurid than the adventures of Nancy, Frank, and Joe. Sweet Valley High, which debuted in 1983, was a soap-opera book series that pitted a manipulative, selfish twin against her good sister. Significantly, these new young adult series books were issued as paperbacks that could be racked, like adult page-turners, in supermarkets and drugstores, and eventually, even Nancy Drew books followed suit. Her books started to look more like adult fare, emblazoned with provocative titles like *Hit and Run Holiday* (1986), *Sinister Paradise* (1988), and *Power of Suggestion* (1993).

When Simon & Schuster took charge, the company figured that Nancy Drew would need a split personality if she was to compete in an increasingly cutthroat market and contribute her fair share to their corporate bottom line. Paperback Nancy Drew Mystery stories, which picked up from the classic hardcover series, featured Nancy at work in spooky gothic environments and were marketed to girls eight to eleven years old. In 1986, a sexier Nancy, as obsessed with romance and clothes as with evil and justice, debuted in *Secrets Can Kill*, the first installment in the new Nancy Drew Files series written for girls in the sixth and seventh grades:

> *Hands on her hips, Nancy Drew stood in the middle of her bedroom and surveyed the situation. New clothes lay everywhere—strewn across the bed, draped over the backs of chairs, and spilling out of shopping bags. Laughing at the mess, Nancy*

BAD, *bad* BOOKS

Until the 1960s, overprotective librarians kept Nancy Drew and Hardy Boys books off their shelves because they believed that kids should read "literature" and not waste their time on the "junk reading."

The Hardy Boys and Nancy Drew have survived threats to their lives in every book, but it was trickier to dodge the slings and arrows directed at them by fussy educators, librarians, and worried parents who criticized the books as dangerous junk reading. Many school administrators, who believed that sensationalized stories about omnipotent children encouraged disrespectfulness, forbade local public schools and libraries to buy series books. Other critics claimed that girls' lives would be warped if they read boys' adventures and that "worthless, sensational books" not only wasted kids' precious reading hours, but encouraged a "perverted reading taste," "sluggishness," and a false sense of reality in America's youth.

The finger-pointing went on for decades. Incensed critics called for series books to be burned; less hotheaded authorities warned against formulaic plots, cardboard characters, and reading matter meant to entertain, not educate. "As some boys read such books," Franklin K. Mathiews, chief librarian of the Boy Scouts of America, wrote in a 1914 article, "Blowing Out the Boy's Brains," "their imaginations are literally 'blown out,' and they go into life as terribly crippled as though by some material explosion they had lost a hand or foot." Unhappy adults had much to rail against; in 1927, 80 percent of books read by American youth were series produced by the Stratemeyer Syndicate.

Naysayers kept series books out of most public libraries until the late 1960s, when concern over dropping reading scores grew extreme enough that librarians and teachers changed their tunes: any book a kid wanted to read was better than none.

reached for a just-bought pair of designer jeans.

"How do you like the new look in private detective?" she said, slipping the jeans on. "Undercover and overdressed!" . . .

Nancy studied herself in the mirror. She liked what she saw. The tight jeans looked great on her long, slim legs and the green sweater complemented her strawberry-blonde hair. Her eyes flashed with the excitement of a new case. She was counting on solving the little mystery fairly easily. In fact, Nancy thought, it would probably be fun! "Right now," she said to her two friends, "the hardest part of this case is deciding what to wear."

Along with an obsession with fashion, modern Nancy Drew volumes feature murder, espionage, altered states, long kisses, and lots of passionate panting.

Soon, Nancy had a third personality. In 1994, to reach a younger audience, there appeared Nancy Drew Notebooks, which featured a grade-school-age Nancy for five- to eight-year-olds. Then, beginning in 1995, still another Nancy went off to Wilder University in the Nancy Drew on Campus series, in which plots touch upon everything from everyday college life to interracial romance. In each of these new series, Nancy sported a different look and point of view; she also shared the slang and concerns of whatever age group she was in at that moment.

The Hardy Boys got the same fragmenting makeover and hormone treatment. There were new Hardy Boys mystery stories in paperback and hardcover, as well as Frank and Joe Hardy: The

Simon & Schuster's two new paperback series, the Nancy Drew Files (1986) and the Hardy Boys Casefiles (1987) were written with readers ages eleven and up in mind. The Hardy Boys deal in computer crime and toxic waste and dabble in virtual reality when they're not looking for their kidnapped girlfriends. Nancy, matured into a sexy detective, experiences heavy doses of danger and romance in her life. Designed to appeal to older girls, mysteries with titles like *Secrets Can Kill* and *Mixed Signals* sported a new Nancy with feathered hair and sultry looks, who finds dead bodies and gorgeous men wherever she goes.

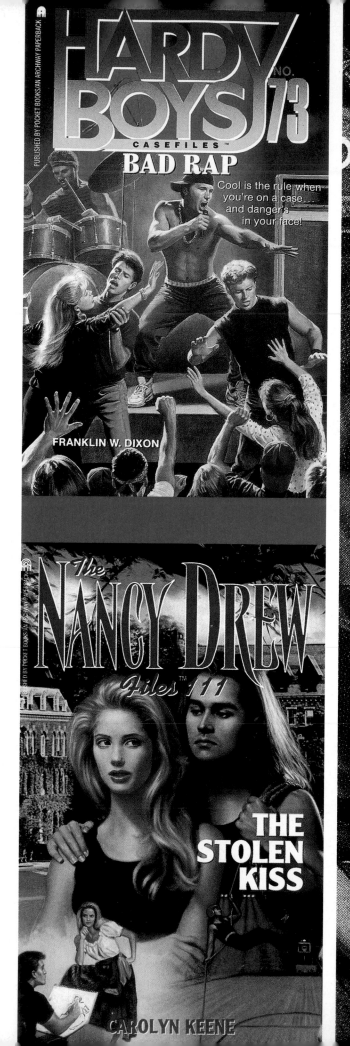

Clues Brothers, introduced in 1997. In the Hardy Boys Casefiles, first issued in 1987, the boys seemed to be paying serious attention to girls for the first time. Some new technological toys were at their disposal, too: answering machines, modems, and police helicopters.

The action in both series shifted from small-town America to a more sophisticated world studded with technopop-blaring international discos, jet-set resorts, spas, fashionable ski slopes, and luxury yachts owned by supermodels. Plots hinged on terrorism, videotape blackmail, stalking, computer theft, cults, vandalism, and manhunts for missing rock stars. African Americans, Native Americans, and gay people emerged from obscurity and became equal-opportunity good guys and upstanding citizens.

Simon & Schuster's game plan worked. By the late 1980s and early 1990s, the teen detectives were mainstays on the best-seller lists of chain bookstores. Today, their cars, crimes, sleuthing techniques, and lifestyles continue to come up to speed, and the Nancy Drew–Hardy Boys universe keeps expanding. Boxed, leather-bound editions and facsimiles of the classic, original-text books in each series are sold to people who revere the characters as both fond memories and literary accomplishments in children's series literature. Collectors and fans hunt down old out-of-print editions of the books. Nancy has inspired theater pieces, ballets, at least one rock band, a tongue-in-cheek lesbian detective series, and Web sites. The Hardy Boys, with their sense of humor, would probably chuckle over the parodies based on their adventures: satires in the *National Lampoon*, a videotape in which they're impersonated by talented dogs, and an avant-garde production of a "Nancy-Boys" mystery, *Murder at Minsing Manor*.

Barely a week goes by without some woman in the news referring to how she was inspired by

FOREVER *young*

Jack LaLanne, octogenarian godfather of the physical fitness movement, flexed his muscles on TV in the 1950s and preached that the way to stay young is through workouts and vitamins.

In 1957, on national television, Mary Martin played the little boy adventurer Peter Pan and defiantly belted out:

> I won't grow up/I don't wanna go to school/Just to learn to be a parrot/And recite the silly rules
> 'Cause growing up is awful-er/Than all the awful things there ever were/I'll never grow up!/Never grow up!/Never grow up!/No, sir!

The snappy song stuck in kids' minds, a second national anthem for the seventy-seven million baby boomers, whose determination to live in Neverland helped hatch a youth culture that transformed everyday life for young and old Americans alike.

Visionary marketing guru Eugene Gilbert was one of the first to identify adolescents as a formidable, untapped economic force in the years following World War II. He noted that with money to spend, teens bought their own movie tickets, cosmetics, clothing, candy bars, beverages, and records, and, with firm ideas about what was cool, influenced what their parents bought, too.

For adults, the end of the Depression and victory in the war meant that the time for sacrifice was over, and they acted like teenagers, too, reveling in a mid-century consumer paradise stocked with yellow refrigerators and two-tone convertibles. Each season's advertisements trumpeted the arrival of "new" and "improved" laundry soaps, sedans, and breakfast cereals, and another thrilling cycle of endless choices.

Taking a tip from Frank Sinatra, who, in 1954, crooned about fairy tales coming true for the young at heart, American consumers sipped from the fountain of youth, donned halter tops and Bermuda shorts, heated up TV dinners, and, with a sense of relief and a tinge of guilt, banished their aging parents to the first retirement colonies. And when they started to age themselves, they sneaked nips of Geritol and washed years and gray hair away with Rinse-Away.

Trade-offs abounded. You could stay young if you kept shopping, you could keep shopping if you kept working, you could keep working if you toed the corporate line. But in the early 1960s, baby-boom teenagers, fearful that Neverland could be blown to smithereens by cold-war Commies, realized that they might never make it to old age. They looked around at the adult world of compromises and conformity, and opted to let their hair grow and to sample a smorgasbord of sex and recreational drugs in pursuit of higher consciousness and less hypocritical, more humanitarian values. If adults had been terrorized by juvenile delinquency in the 1950s, now they had to deal with an influential breed of youthful rebels who mesmerized the media—and advertisers—and were in constant need of new images and stimulations. A trippy counterculture advocated anarchy in fashion, music, home life, education, politics, sexuality, and spirituality. Only one rule governed this groovy reality: "Don't trust anyone over thirty."

Campus riots, ongoing involvement in Vietnam, and the Watergate scandal in the seventies proved conclusively that the grown-ups had blown it. The optimism of the 1960s, from the hippie counterculture to the hope of the civil rights movement, evaporated and left disillusionment in its place. The "do your own thing" ethos of the sixties spawned the hedonistic, selfish "Me Decade." Feeling powerless to change society, many people abandoned activism to work overtime on themselves, regressing through primal therapy to find their "inner child" or piecing together a more youthful version of themselves with face-lifts, liposuction, and hair and breast implants.

Many marriages couldn't stand the strain of partners' self-searching, and divorce rates shot up. Newly swinging singles tried to fit in at discos on Saturday night. Middle-aged men wore leisure suits and gold chains and blow-dried their thinning hair to make it look fuller. Women of all ages squeezed into expensive designer jeans and went braless, trying to look like Farrah Fawcett or any one of the young celebrities who were replacing an older generation of American icons. High culture buckled under to entertainment, irony, and sarcasm, as movie studios ditched serious drama to make millions pumping out simplistic, high-budget, high-tech adventures for children of all ages.

By the 1980s, anyone desperate to look young had options galore. Suntan parlors, collagen shots, and brightly colored running suits could mask differences that had once distinguished one age group from another. Advertisements romanticizing the lives of "senior citizens" and upbeat television comedies like *The Golden Girls* only thinly disguised the country's deep hostility toward the idea of aging. The "look" of age could be bought rather than experienced; Wall Street predators snatched up old and trusted corporate brand names while housewives glazed their walls in faux finishes. In the Reagan era of greed, when successful baby boomers unashamedly crowed, "Whoever wins gets to keep all the toys!," they meant the Rolex watches, the Godiva chocolates, and the black BMWs.

As the century draws to a close, it's now fourteen-year-olds who are the modeling superstars, the unlined, inexperienced yardsticks against which kids and adults alike can't help but measure themselves. Generational lines are blurred: now Gramps, Dad, and Baby all wear their baseball caps backward. And as baby boomers push fifty and snatch glimpses of the end, they're making one last stab at suspending time by flooding America's malls and mail-order catalogs with the nostalgic trappings of the greatest childhood in the history of the human race.

Nancy Drew. Ever since she sprang from Edward Stratemeyer's fertile mind, Nancy Drew has inspired readers to become accomplished at whatever they choose to do, against whatever odds they have to overcome. Many women of accomplishment, from politicians to photojournalists to opera stars and TV anchorwomen, credit Nancy for inspiring in them the guts and determination to reach the top of their professions. The Hardy Boys teach their fans something different, yet just as encouraging—to accept challenges, commit to a course of action, and charge full-steam ahead into life. It's not surprising that academics and commentators research and expound on what makes these characters so much a part of America's mythology and popular culture.

Sales of the Hardy Boys and Nancy Drew remain strong to this day. In the late 1990s, Simon & Schuster had more than 57 million copies of 480 Nancy Drew and Hardy Boys titles in print, not including international editions in over twenty languages, and the Grosset & Dunlap reprints sell briskly, too. And while sales of the books may go up and down from decade to decade—and though Nancy Drew still outsells the Hardy Boys—their shared impact on the kids who read them endures. It makes little difference if one reader, born in 1920, remembers Nancy wearing white gloves, and another, born in 1970, thinks of her in her tight designer jeans, whether men remember the Hardy Boys speeding along on bicycles or on jet skis. In either case, they relive time spent with characters who got into their psyches with a powerful message: that reading can transport kids to exciting worlds of adventure. Who can forget holding a new Hardy Boys or Nancy Drew mystery and studying the cover, then opening it up, feeling the paper, and being drawn into the attention-grabbing swirl of words that start to spin the story?

Reading, especially for kids, is a powerful, transformative experience. It's a way, with the help of a kindly author, to step away from the mundane details of life and to tell a story to yourself. Reading fulfills a hunger we all share, a need to make some sense out of life, and to do it through words—not through the pictures that fly by in movie theaters and on television screens, but with images we develop in our own imaginations, at our own pace. That's an experience only a book can deliver. And while series books have been accused of being volumes of clichés filled with stock characters that waste kids' time, it's undeniable that when a kid chooses a book—any book— it's a step toward a lifetime of reading.

Each mystery that Nancy, Frank, and Joe solve reminds young readers that although the world may be an out-of-control place, good *can* triumph over evil, that the worst problems can be solved if we each do our share and our best to help others. That's a message that leaves no room for indulgence, self-doubt, or hesitation. With all the energy, charm, and arrogance of youth, Nancy, Frank, and Joe live by helping others, an idea that comes and goes in American culture, where just as often we're taught to look out for ourselves alone. As kids we're excited by the adventures in the books; as adolescents we seek out the characters for inspiration; as teens we hope to see some part of ourselves reflected back. And as adults we look back at the eternal teenagers, Nancy Drew and Frank and Joe Hardy, and remember their passion for life, promise, and clarity—and ours, too, when we were young.

It had to happen: Nancy Drew and Hardy Boys Super Mystery books, in which the three sleuths and their respective friends, working on separate cases in the same city, routinely cross paths and join forces. In a rare moment, in *The Last Resort* (1989), Nancy and Frank, stuck in a shack during an avalanche, exchange one tender kiss before they both think better of it.

A NANCY DREW AND HARDY BOYS

NANCY DREW AND HARDY BOYS

SUPER MYSTERY™

Carolyn Keene

Together in an all-new adventure!

Acknowledgments

The Mysterious Case of Nancy Drew and the Hardy Boys would have gone unsolved were it not for the fans and scholars who spent their youths reading the books and their adult lives loving, collecting, and studying the teen sleuths. In a world where so many people are proprietary about information, these people's willingness to share what they knew astounded us. Were it not for their expertise, enthusiasm, and generosity, we would not have been able to bring the story behind Nancy Drew and the Hardy Boys to a larger audience.

On the Hardy Boys front, where serious research is just beginning, we're indebted to Tony Carpentieri, who knows more about Frank and Joe than anyone else on earth except his colleague, Paul Mular, who spent hours answering our questions. Robert Nelson, whose life was changed by reading the books as a child, was cheerful, knowledgeable, and indispensable in helping us crack the Hardy Boys' history and secrets.

We were lucky to find Ilana Nash and Karen Plunkett-Powell, two committed researchers who, when it comes to Nancy Drew, the more frequently studied sleuth, are tops in their field. Their wisdom, perspective, and refreshing humor about Nancy kept us going.

We thank Tony and Mary Carpentieri, Karen Plunkett-Powell, Ilana Nash, and Kate Emburg for loaning us valuable books, memorabilia, and collectibles.

Staff members at the New York Public Library, Manuscripts and Archive Division, who are in the midst of cataloguing a mountain of primary material about the Stratemeyer Syndicate—over five hundred boxes of primary documents, letters, scrapbooks, photographs, and series books—interrupted their meticulous work to help us. Martha Foley, manuscript specialist, is an imaginative archivist who grasped our point of view, dealt with our guerrilla tactics and pressured demands, and even anticipated our needs. Lenya Yurevich, technical assistant, was her patient aide. It was Mary B. Bowling, curator of manuscripts, who agreed to let us have access to material that has not been available to the public. We are immensely grateful.

Investigating a popular-culture subject, especially one steeped in lore and conventional wisdom, is always tricky. We needed a devil's advocate, an expert in the field of children's literature, and James D. Keeline, manager of the Prince and the Pauper Collectible Children's Books in San Diego, was ours. He raised important issues and provided sources and facts that made us more rigorous in our work. We're also thankful to the authors and researchers who preceded us in their work on series books, the Stratemeyer Syndicate, and Nancy, Frank, and Joe: Betsey Caprio, John T. Dizer, Roger Garis, Karen Nelson Hoyle, Deidre Johnson, Bobbie Ann Mason, Gil O'Gara, Karen Plunkett-Powell, and Arthur Prager. Grace Palladino's book, *Teenagers,* was enormously insightful and gave us an intelligent overview of teenage life in America. We also thank Mildred Wirt Benson, the author of the earliest Nancy Drew books, whom we were lucky enough to speak with. We thank her for her reminiscences.

Phyllis Wender, our indefatigable agent, has our gratitude for keeping us sane and the book on track. She introduced us to Simon & Schuster and Bill Rosen, who suggested that we tackle Nancy Drew and the Hardy Boys as our next book project. Throughout this complicated process, Constance Herndon, our editor, has embodied the true spirit of Nancy Drew: intelligent, tough, astute, dependable, and blonde. Anne Greenberg, executive editor of Archway Paperbacks and Minstrel Books, who is responsible for the sleuths in all their Simon & Schuster incarnations, was supportive each step of the way. She made available research that brought the original characters to life, and she helped us understand them as a publishing phenomenon. Additional thanks at Simon & Schuster go to Andrea Au, Edith Baltazar, Janice Easton, Cherlynne Li, Peter McCulloch, Allene Shimomura, Matthew Shine, and Rodger Weinfeld.

This book would have been less fun without the goodwill and spirit of Francesca Richer, our design supervisor, whose professionalism and willingness to pitch in and help us finish the book's design was lifesaving.

As always, our thanks to friends and colleagues at picture agencies for their expertise, patience, and good humor: Michael Shulman, Archive Photos; Jocelyn Clapp, Corbis-Bettmann; Roberta Groves, H. Armstrong Roberts; Ron and Howard Mandelbaum, Photofest. Thanks also to Candice Pryor and the archivists at the YMCA of Greater New York for their kind help, and to Jellybean Photographic Services for their great work on the project.

We can't thank our staff enough for showing grace under pressure and doing such good work. Akiko Takano, our managing editor, is the intelligent voice of reason who made this book happen on schedule. Mira Jacob, assistant editor, researched ideas, coordinated research, and wrote selected pieces about teens' real-world experiences. Sharon Harper, editorial assistant, took charge of details and pictures and was a valued contributor. Susan Jonas and Marilyn Nissenson were the text researchers we relied on, and Paula Glatzer did a superb job commenting on our text; for their solid work we are grateful. Interns Michelle Suh and Johanna Maron did pivotal research in the early stages of the project, and, later, Jackie Schlossman did her valuable share. We also thank Danne Almirall, Keith Daigle, Arfus Greenwood, Frank Kendig, Fred Marshall, Patricia O'Connell, Ray Smith, Alanna Stang, Vickie Woods, and Anne Yarowsky. Finally, special thanks to Maurice Berger, who knows what it takes to do a job fast and well, and to Allan Chasanoff—forgive us for listening to only some of your advice.
—CK/MH

Picture Credits

Selected Bibliography

Carpentieri, Tony, with Paul Mular. *Hardy and Hardy Investigations.* Rheem Valley, Calif.: SynSine Press, 1997.

Cart, Michael. *From Romance to Realism: Fifty Years of Growth and Change in Young Adult Literature.* New York: HarperCollins, 1996.

Children's Literature Research Collections. *Girls Series Books: A Checklist of Titles Published 1840–1991.* Minneapolis: University of Minnesota Libraries, Children's Literature Research Collections, 1992.

Dyer, Carolyn Stewart, and Nancy Tillman Romalov, eds. *Rediscovering Nancy Drew.* Iowa City: University of Iowa Press, 1995.

Farah, David. *Farah's Guide.* Sunland, Calif.: Farah's Books, 1994.

Frank, Thomas. *The Conquest of Cool: Business Culture, Counterculture, and the Rise of Hip Consumerism.* Chicago: University of Chicago Press, 1997.

Giannetti, Charlene C., and Margaret Sagarese. *The Roller-Coaster Years.* New York: Broadway Books, 1997.

Johnson, Deidre. *Edward Stratemeyer and the Stratemeyer Syndicate.* Twayne's United States Authors Series, no. 627. New York: Twayne Publishing, 1993.

Lindsey, Linda L. *Gender Roles: A Sociological Perspective.* Englewood Cliffs, N.J.: Prentice-Hall, 1990.

O'Gara, Gil, ed. *Yellowback Library* (newsletter about series books), vols. 6 (1981); 7–12 (1982); 13–18 (1983); 19 (1984); 25, 28, 30 (1985); 31, 32, 34 (1986); 38, 40 (1987); 43, 48, 50, 54 (1988); 67–72, 74–78 (1990); 79–82, 85, 86 (1991); 97 (1992); 99, 105, 107, 108, 112 (1993); 116–119, 121, 125, 126 (1994); 127, 129, 130, 132 (1995). Des Moines, Iowa: Yellowback Press.

Palladino, Grace. *Teenagers: An American History.* New York: Basic Books, 1996.

Prager, Arthur. *Rascals at Large, or The Clue in the Old Nostalgia.* Garden City, N.Y.: Doubleday, 1971.

Society of Phantom Friends. *The Whispered Watchword* (newsletter), vols. 90-2 (1990); 93-7, 93-10, 93-11 (1993); 94-1 (1994); 95-1, 95-8, 95-10 (1995); 96-3, 96-8, 96-9 (1996); 97-1, 97-2, 97-4, 97-9 (1997). North Highlands, Calif.: Society of Phantom Friends.

The girls held rigid poses as the intruder entered the room